THE KINGFISHER TREASURY OF

Animal Stories

KINGFISHER
a Houghton Mifflin Company imprint
222 Berkeley Street
Boston, Massachusetts 02116
www.houghtonmifflinbooks.com

First published in 1992

2 4 6 8 10 9 7 5 3

2TR/0206/THOM/MA/115IWF

LIBRARY OF CONGRESS CATALOGING-IN-PUBLICATION DATA
The Kingfisher treasury of animal stories / chosen by Jane Olliver; illustrated by Annabel
Spenceley.—1st American ed.
p. cm
Summary: A collection of modern and traditional stories about animals, by such authors as
Aesop, Ted Hughes, and Rudyard Kipling.
1. Animals—Juvenile fiction. 2. Children's stories. 3. Tales.
[1. Animals—Fiction. 2. Short Stories. 3. Animals—Folklore 4. Folklore.]
I. Olliver, Jane. II. Spenceley, Annable, ill.
PZ5.T744 1992
[Fic]—dc20   92-53100   CIP   AC

ISBN 0-7534-5629-X
ISBN 978-07534-5629-3

Printed in India

THE KINGFISHER TREASURY OF
Animal Stories

CHOSEN BY JANE OLLIVER

ILLUSTRATED BY ANNABEL SPENCELEY

KINGFISHER

BOSTON

CONTENTS

THE ELEPHANT'S CHILD

Rudyard Kipling

In the High and Far-Off Times the Elephant, O Best Beloved, had no trunk. He had only a blackish, bulgy nose, as big as a boot, that he could wriggle about from side to side; but he couldn't pick up things with it. But there was one Elephant – a new Elephant – an Elephant's Child – who was full of 'satiable curtiosity, and that means he asked ever so many questions. *And* he lived in Africa, and he filled all Africa with his 'satiable curtiosities. He asked his tall aunt, the Ostrich, why her tail-feathers grew just so, and his tall aunt the Ostrich spanked him with her hard, hard claw. He asked his tall uncle, the Giraffe, what made his skin spotty, and his tall uncle, the Giraffe, spanked him with his hard, hard hoof. And still he was full of 'satiable curtiosity! He asked his broad aunt, the Hippopotamus, why her eyes were red, and his broad aunt, the Hippopotamus, spanked him with her broad, broad hoof; and he asked his hairy uncle, the Baboon, why melons tasted just so, and his hairy uncle, the Baboon, spanked him with his hairy, hairy paw. And *still* he was full of 'satiable curtiosity! He asked questions about everything he saw, or heard, or felt, or smelled, or touched, and all his uncles and his aunts spanked him. And still he was full of 'satiable curtiosity.

One fine morning in the middle of the Precession of the Equinoxes this 'satiable Elephant's Child asked a new fine question that he had never ever asked before. He asked, "What does the Crocodile have for dinner?" Then everybody said, "Hush!" in a loud and dretful tone, and they spanked him immediately and directly, without stopping, for a long time.

By and by, when that was finished, he came upon Kolokolo Bird sitting in the middle of a wait-a-bit thorn bush, and he said, "My father has spanked me, and my mother has spanked me; all my aunts and uncles have spanked me for my 'satiable curtiosity; and *still* I want to know what the Crocodile has for dinner!"

The Kolokolo Bird said, with a mournful cry, "Go to the banks of the great gray-green greasy Limpopo River, all set about with fever-trees, and find out."

That very next morning, when there was nothing left of the Equinoxes, because the Precession had preceded according to precedent, this 'satiable Elephant's Child took a hundred pounds of bananas (the little short red kind), and a hundred pounds of sugarcane (the long purple kind), and seventeen melons (the greeny-crackly kind), and said to all his dear families, "Goodbye. I am going to the great gray-green, greasy Limpopo River, all set about

with fever-trees, to find out what the Crocodile has for dinner." And they all spanked him once more for luck, though he asked them most politely to stop.

Then he went away, a little warm, but not at all astonished. He went from Graham's Town to  Kimberley, and from Kimberley to Khama's Country, and then from Khama's Country he went east by north, eating melons all the time, till at last he came to the banks of the great gray-green, greasy Limpopo River, all set about with fever-trees, precisely as the Kolokolo Bird had said.

Now you must know and understand, O Best Beloved, that till that very week, and day, and hour, and minute, this 'satiable Elephant's Child had never seen a Crocodile, and did not know what one was like. It was all his 'satiable curtiosity.

The first thing that he found was a Bi-Colored-Python-Rock-Snake curled around a rock.

"'Scuse me," said the Elephant's Child politely, "but have you seen such a thing as a Crocodile in these promiscuous parts?"

"*Have* I seen a Crocodile?" said the Bi-Colored-Python-Rock-Snake, in a voice of dretful scorn. "What will you ask me next?"

"'Scuse me," said the Elephant's Child, "but could you kindly tell me what he has for dinner?"

Then the Bi-Colored-Python-Rock-Snake uncoiled himself very quickly from the rock, and spanked the Elephant's Child with his scalesome, flailsome tail.

"That is odd," said the Elephant's Child, "because my father and my mother, and my uncle and my aunt, not to mention my other aunt, the Hippopotamus, and my other uncle, the Baboon, have all spanked me for my 'satiable curtiosity – and I suppose this is the same thing."

So he said good-bye very politely to the Bi-Colored-Python-Rock-Snake, and helped to coil him up on the rock again, and went on, a little warm, but not at all astonished, eating melons, and throwing the rind about, because he could not pick it up, till he trod on what he thought was a log of wood at the very edge of the great gray-green, greasy Limpopo River, all set about with fever-trees.

But it was really the Crocodile, O Best Beloved,

and the Crocodile winked one eye – like this!

"'Scuse me," said the Elephant's Child politely, "but do you happen to have seen a Crocodile in these promiscuous parts?"

Then the Crocodile winked the other eye, and lifted half of his tail out of the mud; and the Elephant's Child stepped back most politely, because he did not wish to be spanked again.

"Come hither, Little One," said the crocodile. "Why do you ask such things?"

"'Scuse me," said the Elephant's Child most politely, "but my father has spanked me, my mother has spanked me, not to mention my tall aunt, the Ostrich, and my tall uncle, the Giraffe, who can kick ever so hard, as well as my broad aunt, the Hippopotamus, and my hairy uncle, the Baboon, *and* including the Bi-Colored-Python-Rock-Snake, with the scalesome tail, just up the bank, who spanks harder than any of them; and *so*, if it's all the same to you, I don't want to be spanked any more."

"Come hither, Little One," said the Crocodile, "for I am the crocodile," and he wept crocodile tears to show it was quite true.

Then the Elephant's Child grew all breathless, and panted, and kneeled down on the bank and said, "You are the very person I have been looking for all these long days. Will you tell me what you have for dinner?"

"Come hither, Little One," said the Crocodile, "and I'll whisper."

Then the Elephant's Child put his head down
close to the Crocodile's musky, tusky mouth, and
the Crocodile caught him by his little nose, which
up to that very day, hour, and minute, had been no
bigger than a boot, though much more useful.

"I think," said the Crocodile — and he said it
between his teeth, like this, "I think today I will
begin with the Elephant's Child!"

At this, O Best Beloved, the Elephant's Child was
much annoyed, and he said, speaking through his
nose, like this, "Led go! You are hurtig be!"

Then the Bi-Colored-Python-Rock-Snake scuffled down from the bank and said "My young
friend, if you do not now, immediately and instantly, pull as hard as ever you can, it is my opinion
that your acquaintance in the large-pattern leather

16

ulster" (and by this he meant the Crocodile) "will jerk you into yonder limpid stream before you can say Jack Robinson."

This is the way Bi-Colored-Python-Rock-Snakes always talk.

Then the Elephant's Child sat back on his little haunches, and pulled, and pulled, and pulled, and his nose began to stretch. And the Crocodile floundered into the water, making it all creamy with great sweeps of his tail, and *he* pulled, and pulled, and pulled.

Then the Elephant's Child felt his legs slipping, and he said through his nose, which was now nearly five feet long, "This is too butch for be!"

Then the Bi-Colored-Python-Rock-Snake came down from the bank, and knotted himself in a double-clove-hitch around the Elephant's Child's hind legs, and said, "Rash and inexperienced traveler, we will now seriously devote ourselves to a little high tension, because if we do not, it is my impression that yonder self-propelling man-of-war with the armor-plated upper deck" (and by this, O Best Beloved, he meant the Crocodile) "will permanently vitiate your future career."

That is the way Bi-Colored-Python-Rock-Snakes always talk.

So he pulled, and the Elephant's Child pulled, and the Crocodile pulled; but the Elephant's Child and the Bi-Colored-Python-Rock-Snake pulled hardest; and at last the Crocodile let go of the Elephant's Child's nose with a plop that you could hear all up and down the Limpopo.

Then the Elephant's Child sat down most hard and sudden; but first he was careful to say "Thank you" to the Bi-Colored-Python-Rock-Snake; and next he was kind to his poor pulled nose, and wrapped it all up in cool banana leaves, and hung it in the great gray-green, greasy Limpopo to cool.

"What are you doing that for?" said the Bi-Colored-Python-Rock-Snake.

"'Scuse me," said the Elephant's Child, "but my nose is badly out of shape, and I am waiting for it to shrink."

"Then you will wait a long time," said the Bi-Colored-Python-Rock-Snake. "Some people do not know what is good for them."

The Elephant's Child sat there for three days waiting for his nose to shrink. But it never grew any shorter, and, besides, it made him squint. For, O Best Beloved, you will see and understand that the Crocodile had pulled it out into a really truly trunk the same as all Elephants have today.

At the end of the third day a fly came and stung him on the shoulder, and before he knew what he was doing he lifted up his trunk and hit that fly dead with the end of it.

"'Vantage number one!" said the Bi-Colored-Python-Rock-Snake. "You couldn't have done that with a mere-smear nose. Try and eat a little now."

Before he thought what he was doing the Elephant's Child put out his trunk and plucked a large bundle of grass, dusted it clean against his forelegs, and stuffed it into his own mouth.

"'Vantage number two!" said the Bi-Colored-Python-Rock-Snake. "You couldn't have done that with a mere-smear nose. Don't you think the sun is very hot here?"

"It is," said the Elephant's Child, and before he thought what he was doing he schlooped up a schloop of mud from the banks of the great gray-green, greasy Limpopo, and slapped it on his head, where it made a cool schloopy-sloshy mud-cap.

"'Vantage number three!" said the Bi-Colored-Python-Rock-Snake. "You couldn't have done that with a mere-smear nose. Now how do you feel about being spanked again?"

"Oh dear," said the Elephant's Child, "I should not like it at all."

"How would you like to spank somebody?" said the Bi-Colored-Python-Rock-Snake.

"I should like it very much indeed," said Elephant's Child.

"Well," said the Bi-Colored-Python-Rock-Snake, "you will find that new nose of yours very useful to spank people with."

So the Elephant's Child went home across Africa frisking and whisking his trunk. When he wanted fruit to eat he pulled fruit down from a tree, instead of waiting for it to fall as he used to. When he wanted grass he plucked grass up from the ground, instead of going on his knees as he used to do. When the flies bit him he broke off the branch of a tree and used it as a fly whisk; and he made himself a new, cool, slushy-squshy mud-cap whenever the sun was hot. When he felt lonely walking through Africa he sang to himself down his trunk, and the noise was louder than several brass bands. He went specially out of his way to find a broad Hippopotamus (she was no relation of his), and he spanked her very

hard, to make sure that the Bi-Colored-Python-Rock-Snake had spoken the truth about his new trunk. The rest of the time he picked up the melon-rinds that he had dropped on his way to the Limpopo – for he was a Tidy Pachyderm.

One dark evening he came back to all his dear families, and he coiled up his trunk and said, "How do you do?" They were very glad to see him, and immediately said, "Come here and be spanked for your 'satiable curtiosity."

"Pooh," said the Elephant's Child. "I don't think you people know anything about spanking; but *I* do, and I'll show you."

Then he uncurled his trunk and knocked two of his dear brothers head over heels.

"O Bananas!" said they, "where did you learn that trick, and what have you done to your nose?"

"I got a new one from the Crocodile on the banks of the great, gray-green, greasy Limpopo River," said the Elephant's Child. "I asked him what he had for dinner, and he gave me this to keep."

"It looks very ugly," said his hairy uncle, the Baboon.

"It does," said the Elephant's Child. "But it's very useful," and he picked up his hairy uncle, the Baboon, by one hairy leg, and hove him into a hornets' nest.

Then that bad Elephant's Child spanked all his dear families for a long time, till they were very warm and greatly astonished. He pulled out his tall

Ostrich aunt's tail-feathers; and he caught his tall uncle, the Giraffe, by the hind leg, and dragged him through a thorn bush; and he shouted at his broad aunt, the Hippopotamus, and blew bubbles into her ear when she was sleeping in the water.

At last things grew so exciting that his dear families went off one by one in a hurry to the banks of the great gray-green, greasy Limpopo River, all set about with fever-trees, to borrow new noses from the Crocodile. When they came back nobody spanked anybody any more; and ever since that day, O Best Beloved, all the Elephants you will ever see, beside all those that you won't, have trunks precisely like the trunk of the 'satiable Elephant's Child.

THE HARE AND THE TORTOISE

Aesop

It was a cold winter's night. It was snowing on the rooftops and on the streets. It was snowing on the forests and on the fields. The birds had taken to their nests, the badgers huddled together in their sets, and foxes lay shivering in their dens. Somewhere, in a warm, cosy bed in a warm, cosy room in a warm, cosy house, lay a warm, cosy little girl. Beside the bed sat her father who was about to read her a story. This is how it began:

"Once upon a time . . ."

"When was it, Daddy?" asked the little girl. She asked a lot of questions.

"When this story began, love. Now don't interrupt, please. Once upon a time," he went on quickly, "in the middle of the forest, a hare bumped into a tortoise. The hare took one look at the tortoise and burst out laughing.

'What a ridiculous creature you are,' he said.

25

'Look at your funny little legs and your funny little head poking out of that great, heavy shell you hump about on your back. It's a wonder you can move at all.'

'That's most unkind,' Tortoise said, sniffing. He was very hurt but he was not going to cry. 'If you think you're so much better than me, why don't you prove it? We could have a race. Yes, that's it: I challenge you to a race!'

'A race. Ha, ha, ha! Why, you wouldn't stand a chance!' Hare giggled. 'It'd be a complete waste of time; like pitting a tortoise against a hare.' He thought this was a tremendous joke.

'You can laugh, Hare, you can laugh. Just you wait.'

But Hare only laughed even louder, so Tortoise decided to be rude to him.

'Of course, if you daren't risk it, big ears . . .'

Hare stopped laughing and rose to his full height.

'Dare! Me dare race you, you cheeky little hard-topped toad! I'll show you.'

So the following day Hare and Tortoise went to the middle of the forest to start their race. Hare had invited all his friends to come and watch. They stood by the starting-line and laughed at Tortoise. Tortoise ignored them.

Hare ran like the wind. Tortoise crawled along at a snail's pace. By the time hare came into sight of the finishing-post, Tortoise was still in sight of the start.

'I might as well sit down here for an hour or two,' thought Hare out loud. 'This is very boring. It'll be much more fun if Tortoise actually sees me finish. I can't wait to see the look on his face!'

Hare lay down under a tree and waited. He waited for ages and ages, until it felt as though he had been waiting for ever. In the end he decided to have a snooze. It would pass the time nicely.

He was woken by the sound of great waves crashing against the rocks. Hare rubbed his eyes and looked toward the finishing-post. Then he realized that the waves weren't waves at all.

Hundreds of animals had gathered at the finish and every single one of them was cheering on

Tortoise. He was going to win. By the time Hare came haring up behind him it was too late. Tortoise had already crossed the line.

'Oh, Hare,' chortled Rabbit, 'fancy losing a race to a tortoise!'

'What a joke!' screeched Squirrel, pointing at Hare.

'A disgrace! Shocking! Not fit to be called a hare!' muttered all the other hares and refused to speak to him. Hare hung his head. He wished he had never been born.

'That'll teach him,' murmured Mole.

'Quite,' agreed Owl. 'Pride comes before a fall.'

All the birds began to sing 'For he's a jolly good Tortoise' and the rest of the animals joined in. Tortoise beamed with delight.

'Slow but sure,' he kept saying. 'Slow but sure.' It was the happiest day of his life."

"There," said the little girl's father, closing the book. "What did you think of that? Served old Hare right, didn't it?"

"Mmmm," she replied rather dreamily. Secretly she felt rather sorry for Hare.

"Time to sleep now." Her father kissed her.

"Goodnight," she mumbled into her pillow.

The little girl slowly drifted into sleep. She was thinking about the story. It did seem extraordinary

that the tortoise won, no matter how careless the hare was. After all, tortoises *are* very slow.

As soon as she was asleep she began to dream. As soon as she began to dream she met an old man with a long white beard who looked very sad.

"Why are you sad, old man?" she asked.

"Why am I sad? Anyone in my position would be sad."

He stared fiercely at the little girl who was pestering him, so she waited patiently for him to explain what his position was. She had to be patient because it was a long time before he spoke.

"I'll tell you why I'm sad," he said at last. "They've stolen all my stories, that's why. They were all stories about animals I know. Friends of mine, you might say. People stole the stories and changed them. Gave them meanings I didn't mean at all. They even call them Aesop's Fables now.

As though they weren't even true. Might just as well call them Aesop's Fibs."

"What's Aesop?" asked the little girl.

"Me, silly. I'm Aesop. Didn't they even tell you that? They'll be pretending that I don't exist next. Really!"

Aesop went very red in the face and looked as if he was going to explode. Then he looked sad again.

"Perhaps it's better that way. Better to be incognito."

"What's ink-hog-thingummy?"

"You do ask a lot of questions, don't you? Incognito means that nobody knows who you are."

The little girl was still confused. "I'm afraid that I don't really understand about your stories. How can a story be changed?"

The old man looked at her and shook his head.

"Don't children learn anything these days? Honestly. Oh, alright then. I might as well explain. Let's take an example. Do you know the story of the tortoise and the hare?"

"Yes I do. My daddy just read it to me."

"Well I bet I know how the story went," said Aesop gloomily.

"Why, the tortoise won because the stupid old hare fell asleep," said the little girl.

"And everyone said that it served Hare right," sighed Aesop.

"That's right," she replied. "How did you know?"

"Because I wrote the story, of course. Except that it wasn't like that at all. Do you want me to tell you what really happened?"

"Oh, yes please," she said eagerly.

"Well it was like this," began Aesop. "One day, Hare was skipping through the woods enjoying himself. He usually did."

"He usually did what?" asked the little girl.

"Enjoy himself. I just said so. Now don't start interrupting. Where was I? Oh yes, there was Hare, having a good time in the woods, when up came Badger.

'Hello, Hare,' boomed Badger. 'You're just the chap I wanted to see. There's a bit of a problem with Tortoise and I think you might be able to help.'

'I'd be delighted to,' replied Hare, who was extremely kindhearted and only slightly mad.

'Poor old Tortoise is very unhappy, poor chap. Thinks he's slow and dull, which he is of course, but it's not his fault; it's what comes of being a tortoise. Me and the others, Mole, Owl, Rabbit, and the rest, think he needs a bit of a boost. Which is where you come in.'

'I come in?' frowned Hare.

'Yes. You see, Tortoise is always going on about you. He says you're so lucky, always smiling and leaping around without a care in the world. You're

so easygoing and athletic – everything he's not. So we thought you should have a race together.'

'A race? You mean a running race?' asked Hare, unable to believe his ears; he was so much faster than Tortoise that he couldn't at all see how a race would help.

'A running race, exactly,' repeated Badger, rubbing his big paws together. 'Only you let Tortoise win. Of course, you can't just run slower than he does. That would be impossible, except for a snail. But you can make a mistake, get lost, run into a tree and knock yourself out, anything to make Tortoise think he beat you because he's got something you haven't. Not speed, certainly, but endurance and a sense of direction. Should cheer the old reptile up no end. If you don't mind, that is.'

'Not at all,' beamed Hare. 'Great idea, yippee!' And he leaped around with pleasure at the thought of making Tortoise happy.

'But I shan't knock myself out, if you don't mind. Not necessary and very painful. I've got it. I'll pretend to need a rest and fall asleep. That'll give him time to finish.'

And that's the way it happened. Tortoise only just won so it really did look as if Hare was trying. Tortoise was overjoyed and Hare was the first to congratulate him.

'Well done, Tortoise, well done. It just goes to show that speed isn't everything.'

'Quite,' agreed Badger, slapping Tortoise on the

back. 'Ouch, ow and ouch!' It was a very hard shell. 'Slow but sure, slow but sure, that's my Tortoise,' he added, shaking his injured paw.

'You're all too kind,' said Tortoise, who was blushing so much that even his shell seemed to go red. 'It was nothing really.'

Tortoise never knew how right he was."

"So there it is, young lady," said Aesop, "the true story of the tortoise and the hare. It's been surprisingly nice talking to you, I must say. I feel much better now."

Aesop looked at his watch.

"Heavens, just look at the time. I must be off at once. I'm already late for someone else's dream."

And without more ado the old man vanished.

"Hmmm," thought the little girl, when he had gone, "I don't know what to think anymore. But I know one thing: it's not who wins that counts, it's who tells the story."

She smiled to herself and started another dream.

WHY THE RAVEN HAS BLACK FEATHERS

A North American Tale

Long ago, the raven was a handsome bird with snow-white feathers and magic powers. One day, he saw some people chewing tree roots and digging in the dusty earth for food.

"I must help them," he thought, and flew down to them calling, "Caw! Caw! Caw!"

The people saw him and shouted, "Here is Put-it-Right-Raven! Perhaps he will help us find some food."

The raven picked up a few dry leaves and scattered them on a small pond. Immediately, the water began to hubble and bubble, the leaves vanished and dozens of fish jumped in the water, their silvery sides gleaming in the sun.

The people were thrilled. They had a good meal

of fish, but when they had finished, they realized that their pond had dried up. So they asked Put-it-Right-Raven to help them again.

The raven could find only one well in the whole world. It was in the house of a man called Ganook, but Ganook would not give any of his water away.

The raven thought he might be able to drink enough water to carry back to his friends. He flew to Ganook's house and begged Ganook for a drink of water.

"I can spare only three sips," said Ganook, "so don't drink any more than that." And he showed the raven his well.

The raven sipped, and then tried to gulp. But he began to wobble and Ganook saw him.

"Stop that, Raven," he cried. "Do you want to drink my well dry?"

That was exactly what the raven wanted to do. But instead he said, "Ganook, I shall tell you a story." So they settled down comfortably and the raven began: "It was a dark and stormy night when the chief said to his storyteller, 'Storyteller, tell me a story.' So the storyteller began: 'It was a dark and stormy night when the chief said to his storyteller, 'Storyteller, tell me a story.' So the storyteller began . . .''

The raven's voice was slow and gentle. Over and over again he started the story until Ganook began to doze. As soon as Ganook's eyes were closed, the

raven dashed to the well and started to drink, but Ganook was not quite asleep.

"Get on with the story," he said. "I am not asleep." Then he opened one eye and cried, "Where are you, Raven?"

"Just stretching my legs," the raven answered, and his voice droned on and on: "It was a dull and dreary night when the chief said to his storyteller, 'Snore, snore, snore,'" and that is just what Ganook finally did!

Quietly, the raven went to the well again. Glub, slurp, gulp! He drank every last drop of water, but as he closed his beak, Ganook woke up.

"You've tricked me!" yelled Ganook. "I'll teach you to steal my water." And he seized a stick to beat the raven. Flapping his wings, the raven flew up the chimney. But he was so full of water that he got stuck. Ganook stoked up the fire so that smoke rose up the chimney. The smoke made the poor raven choke and turned his snow-white feathers quite black. He struggled and struggled until at last he heaved himself out of the top of the chimney. Then he flew off, barely able to keep above the trees of the forest he was so weighed down by the water.

As the raven flew, drops of water fell from his beak and made rivers and lakes of fresh, cool water on the Earth. Thanks to the raven's courage, the people never lacked water again. But ever since then, his feathers have been as black as soot.

THE SEVEN FAMILIES OF LAKE PIPPLE-POPPLE

Edward Lear

In former days – that is to say, once upon a time, there lived in the Land of Gramblamble, Seven Families. They lived by the side of the great Lake Pipple-Popple (one of the Seven Families, indeed, lived *in* the Lake), and on the outskirts of the City of Tosh, which, excepting when it was quite dark, they could see plainly. The names of all these places you have probably heard of, and you have only not to look in your geography books to find out all about them.

Now the Seven Families who lived on the borders of the great Lake Pipple-Popple were as follows. There was a family of two old Parrots and seven young Parrots. There was a Family of two old Storks and seven young Storks. There was a Family of two old Geese and seven young Geese. There was a Family of two old Owls and seven young Owls. There was a Family of two old Guinea Pigs and seven young Guinea Pigs. There was a Family of two old Cats and seven young Cats. And there was a Family of two old Fishes and seven young Fishes.

The Parrots lived upon the Soffsky-Poffsky trees – which were beautiful to behold, and covered with blue leaves – and they fed upon fruit, artichokes, and striped beetles.

The Storks walked in and out of Lake Pipple-Popple and ate frogs for breakfast and buttered toast for tea; but on account of the extreme length of their legs, they could not sit down, so they walked about continually.

The Geese, having webs to their feet, caught quantities of flies, which they ate for dinner.

The Owls anxiously looked after mice, which they caught and made into sago puddings.

The Guinea Pigs toddled about the gardens, and ate lettuce and Cheshire cheese.

The Cats sat still in the sunshine, and fed upon sponge cookies.

The Fish lived in the Lake, and fed on periwinkles.

And all these Seven Families lived together in the utmost fun and felicity.

One day all the Seven Fathers and the Seven Mothers of the Seven Families agreed that they would send their children out to see the world.

So they called them all together, and gave them each eight shillings and some good advice, some

chocolate drops, and a small green morocco book to set down their expenses in. They then particularly entreated them not to quarrel, and all the parents sent off their children with a parting injunction.

"If," said the old Parrots, "you find a cherry, do not fight about who shall have it."

"And," said the old Storks, "if you find a frog, divide it carefully into seven bits, and on no account quarrel about it."

And the old Geese said
to the seven young Geese,
"Whatever you do, be
sure you do not touch a
Plum-pudding Flea."

And the old Owls said,
"If you find a mouse, tear
him up into seven slices,
and eat him cheerfully,
but without quarreling."

And the old Guinea
Pigs said, "Have a care
that you eat your lettuce,
should you find any, not
greedily but calmly."

And the old Cats said, "Be particularly careful not
to meddle with a clangle-wangle, if you should see
one."

And the old Fishes said, "Above all things avoid
eating a blue boss-woss, for they do not agree with
fishes, and give them a pain in their toes."

So all the Children of each Family thanked their
parents, and making forty-nine polite bows, they
went into the wide world.

The seven young Parrots had not gone far, when
they saw a tree with a single cherry on it, which the
oldest Parrot picked instantly, but the other six
being extremely hungry, tried to get it also. On
which all the Seven began to fight, and they

scuffled, and huffled, and ruffled, and shuffled, and
puffled, and muffled, and buffled, and duffled, and
fluffled, and guffled, and bruffled, and screamed,
and shrieked, and squealed, and squeaked, and
clawed, and snapped, and bit, and bumped, and
thumped, and dumped, and flumped each other, till
they were all torn into little bits, and at last there was
nothing left to record this painful incident, except
the Cherry and seven small green feathers.

And that was the vicious and voluble end of the
seven young Parrots.

When the seven young Storks set out, they walked or flew for fourteen weeks in a straight line, and for six weeks more in a crooked one; and after that they ran as hard as they could for one hundred and eight miles; and after that they stood still and made a himmeltanious chatter-clatter-blattery noise with their bills.

About the same time they perceived a large Frog, spotted with green, and with a sky-blue stripe under each ear. So being hungry, they immediately flew at him and were going to divide him into seven pieces, when they began to quarrel as to which of his legs should be taken off first. One said this, and another said that, and while they were all quarreling the Frog hopped away. And when they saw that he was gone, they began to chatter-clatter, blatter-platter, patter-blatter, matter-clatter, flatter-quatter, more violently than ever.

And after they had fought for a week they pecked each other to little pieces, so that at last nothing was left of any of them except their bills.

And that was the end of the seven young Storks.

When the seven young Geese began to travel, they went over a large plain, on which there was but one tree, and that was a very bad one. So four of them went up to the top of it, and looked about them, while the other three waddled up and down, and repeated poetry, and their last six lessons in Arithmetic, Geography, and Cookery.

Presently they perceived, a long way off, an object of the most interesting and obese appearance, having a perfectly round body, exactly resembling a plum-pudding, with two little wings and a beak, three feathers growing out of his head and only one leg.

So after a time all the seven young Geese said to

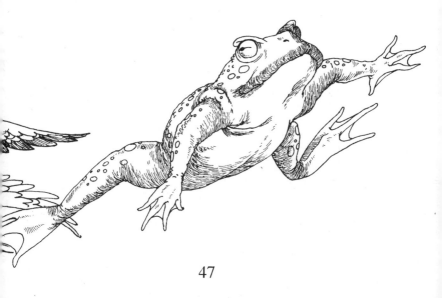

each other, "Beyond all doubt this beast must be a Plum-pudding Flea!" And no sooner had they said this than the Plum-pudding Flea began to hop and skip on his one leg with the most dreadful velocity, and came straight to the tree, where he stopped and looked about him in a vacant and voluminous manner.

On which the seven young Geese were greatly alarmed, and all of a tremble-bemble: so one of them put out his long neck and just touched him with the tip of his bill – but no sooner had he done this than the Plum-pudding Flea skipped and hopped about more and more and higher and higher, after which he opened his mouth, and to the great surprise and indignation of the seven Geese, began to bark so loudly and furiously and terribly that they were totally unable to bear the noise, and by degrees every one of them suddenly tumbled down quite dead.

So that was the end of the seven young Geese.

When the seven young Owls set out, they sat every now and then on the branches of old trees, and never went far at one time. One night when it was quite dark, they thought they heard a mouse, but as the gas lamps were not lighted, they could not see him. So they called out,

"Is that a mouse?"

On which a mouse answered, "Squeaky-peeky-weeky, yes it is."

And immediately all the young Owls threw themselves off the tree, meaning to alight on the ground; but they did not perceive that there was a large well below them, into which they all fell superficially, and where every one of them drowned in less than half a minute.

So that was the end of the seven young Owls.

The seven young Guinea Pigs went into a garden full of Gooseberry-bushes and Tiggory-trees, under one of which they fell asleep. When they awoke they saw a large lettuce which had grown out of the ground while they had been sleeping, and which had an immense number of green leaves. At which they all exclaimed,

> "Lettuce! O Lettuce!
> Let us, O Let us,
> O Lettuce leaves,
> O let us leave this tree and eat
> Lettuce, O let us, Lettuce leaves!"

And instantly the seven young Guinea Pigs rushed with such extreme force against the lettuce plant, and hit their heads so vividly against its stalk, that the concussion brought on directly an incipient transitional inflammation of their noses, which grew worse and worse and worse and worse till it incidentally killed them all seven.

And that was the end of the seven young Guinea Pigs.

The Seven young Cats set off on their travels with great delight and rapacity. But, on coming to the top of a high hill, they perceived at a long distance off a Clangle-Wangle, and in spite of the warning they had had, they ran straight up to it. (Now the Clangle-Wangle is a most dangerous and delusive beast, and by no means commonly to be met with. They live in the water as well as on land, using their long tail as a sail when in the former element. Their speed is extreme, but their habits of life are domestic and superfluous, and their general demeanour pensive and pellucid.)

The moment the Clangle-Wangle saw the seven young Cats approach, he ran away; and he ran straight on for four months, and the Cats, though they continued to run, could never overtake him – they all gradually died of fatigue and exhaustion.

And this was the end of the seven young Cats.

The seven young Fishes swam across the Lake Pipple-Popple and into the river, and into the ocean, where most unhappily for them, they saw, on the fifteenth day of their travels, a bright-blue Boss-Woss, and instantly swam after him. But the Blue Boss-Woss plunged into a perpendicular, spicular,

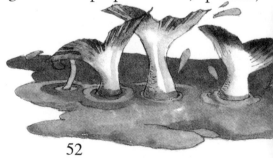

orbicular, quadrangular, circular depth of soft mud, where in fact his house was.

And the seven young Fishes, swimming with great and uncomfortable velocity, plunged also into the mud, quite against their will, and not being accustomed to it, were all suffocated.

And that was the end of the seven young Fishes.

After it was known that the seven young Parrots, and the seven young Storks, and the seven young Geese, and the seven young Owls, and the seven young Guinea Pigs, and the seven young Cats, and the seven young Fishes were all dead, then the Frog, and the Plum-pudding Flea, and the Mouse, and the Clangle-Wangle, and the Blue Boss-Woss, all met to rejoice over their good fortune.

And they collected the seven Feathers of the seven young Parrots, and the seven Bills of the seven young Storks, and the lettuce, and the cherry, and having placed the latter on the lettuce, and the other objects in a circular arrangement at their base, they danced a hornpipe around all these memorials until they were quite tired; then returned to their respective homes full of joy and respect, sympathy, satisfaction, and disgust.

BRER RABBIT GETS HIMSELF A HOUSE

Joel Chandler Harris

Long ago an old man called Uncle Remus used to tell stories to a little boy. The two of them lived on a plantation in the South, and the stories were always about certain animals, Brer Rabbit and Brer Fox in particular, but several others, too, Brer Bear and Brer Possum for instance.

One evening, Uncle Remus ate his supper as usual and then looked at the child over his spectacles and said, "Now then, honey, I'll just rustle around with my memories and see if I can call to mind how old Brer Rabbit got himself a two-story house without paying much for it."

He paused a moment, then told the following story:

It turned out one time that a whole lot of creatures decided to build a house together. Old Brer Bear he was among them, and Brer Fox and Brer Wolf and Brer Coon and Brer Possum, and possibly Brer

Mink too. Anyway, there was a whole bunch of them, and they set to work and built a house in less than no time. Brer Rabbit, he pretended it made his head swim to climb the scaffolding, and that it made him feel dizzy to work in the sun, but he got a board, and he stuck a pencil behind his ear and he went around measuring and marking, measuring and marking.

He looked so busy that all the other creatures were sure he was doing the most work, and folks going along the road said, "My, my, that Brer Rabbit is doing more work than the whole lot of them put together." Yet all the time Brer Rabbit

was doing nothing, and he had plenty of time to lie in the shade scratching fleas off himself.

Meanwhile, the other creatures, they built the house, and it sure was a fine one. It had an upstairs and a downstairs, and chimneys all around, and it had rooms for all the creatures who had helped to make it.

Brer Rabbit, he picked out one of the upstairs rooms, and he got a gun and a brass cannon, and when no one was looking he put them up in the room. Then he got a big bowl of dirty water and carried it up there when no one was looking.

When the house was finished and all the animals were sitting in the parlor after supper, Brer Rabbit, he got up and stretched himself, and made excuses, saying he believed he'd go to his room. When he got there, and while all the others were laughing and chatting and being sociable downstairs, Brer Rabbit stuck his head out of the room and hollered:

"When a big man wants to sit down, whereabouts is he going to sit?" says he.

The other creatures laughed and called back, "If a big man like you can't sit in a chair, he'd better sit on the floor."

"Watch out, down there," says old Brer Rabbit, "because I'm going to sit down," says he.

With that *bang!* went Brer Rabbit's gun. The other creatures looked around at one another in astonishment as much as to say, "What in the name of gracious is that?"

They listened and they listened, but they didn't hear any more fuss and it wasn't long before they were all chatting again.

Then Brer Rabbit stuck his head out of his room again, and hollered, "When a big man like me wants to sneeze, whereabouts is he going to sneeze?"

The other creatures called back, "A big man like you can sneeze anywhere he wants."

"Watch out down there, then," says Brer Rabbit, "because I'm going to sneeze right here," says he.

With that Brer Rabbit let off his cannon – *bulder-um-m-m!* The window panes rattled. The whole house shook as though it would come down, and old Brer Bear fell out of his rocking chair – *kerblump?*

When they all settled down again Brer Possum and Brer Mink suggested that as Brer Rabbit had such a bad cold they would step outside and get some fresh air. The other creatures said that they would stick it out, and before long they all got their hair smoothed down and began to talk again.

After a while, when they were beginning to enjoy themselves once more, Brer Rabbit hollered out:

"When a big man like me chews tobacco, where is he going to spit?"

The other creatures called back as though they were getting pretty angry:

"Big man or little man, spit where you please!"

Then Brer Rabbit called out, "This is the way a big man spits," and with that he tipped over the bowl of dirty water, and when the other creatures heard it come sloshing down the stairs, my, how they rushed out of the house! Some went out the back door, some went out the front door, some fell out of the windows, some went one way and some another way; but they all got out as quickly as they could.

Then Brer Rabbit, he shut up the house, and fastened the windows and went to bed. He pulled the covers up around his ears, and he slept like a man who doesn't owe anybody anything.

"And neither did he owe them," said Uncle Remus to the little boy, "for if the other creatures got scared and ran off from their own house, what business is that of Brer Rabbit? That's what I'd like to know."

THE SEAL CATCHER

A Scottish Tale

In a wild and lonely place on the rocky coast of Scotland, there once lived a man who made his living by catching seals and selling their skins.

One sunny day, the seal catcher came out of his cottage and saw a large seal on the rocks below. Thinking of all the money he could earn from such a fine seal skin, he crept down toward the seal and leaped upon it with his knife.

The rocks were covered with slimy seaweed and the seal catcher slipped just as he stabbed at the seal. With a scream of pain, the seal dived back into the water with the seal catcher's hunting knife still sticking into its side.

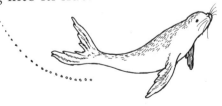

The seal catcher set off home, feeling annoyed at having lost the seal, not to mention his hunting knife. On the way, he met a tall, richly dressed stranger on a magnificent gray horse. He stood aside to let the stranger pass, but, to his surprise, the stranger stopped and asked him what his trade was.

"I'm a seal catcher," he replied. At once, the stranger ordered a hundred seal skins. The seal catcher was delighted at his good fortune until the stranger said, "You must deliver all the seal skins to me tonight."

"But that's impossible!" cried the seal catcher. "The seals won't come back to the rocks again until tomorrow morning. And besides, I have lost my best hunting knife."

"Never mind about that," replied the stranger. "Get up behind me on my horse. I'll take you to where there are hundreds of seals and I'll give you a new knife too."

So the seal catcher got up on the horse behind the stranger and away they went. They rode so fast that they seemed to fly through the air. Suddenly, they came to a stop. They had reached the edge of a steep cliff. Dismounting, they looked down at the foaming sea far below.

The seal catcher looked anxiously around and asked, "Where are the seals you told me about?" He began to feel afraid of the tall stranger and tried to run from him. But the stranger caught him in a firm grip and leaped with him over the cliff edge. Together they plunged down into the sea.

The seal catcher found they were in a strange underwater world where he could breathe as easily as if he were on dry land. He saw that the stranger had changed into a seal. Then he realized that he too had been transformed into a seal.

"There is a spell on me," thought the seal catcher. "Now I will have to remain a seal for the rest of my life."

The stranger took him through an arch in the rocks into a huge cavern where there were hundreds of seals. They looked sad, and many of them were weeping.

"Wait here," said the stranger. Then he went through a hole at the end of the cavern and returned with a knife.

"Is this yours?" he asked sternly.

"It is," mumbled the seal catcher. "But I was only trying to earn my living."

Now the seal catcher thought he understood why he had been brought here. The seals were going to take their revenge and kill him with his own knife. But, instead, they crowded around him, gently rubbing their soft noses against him.

"Follow me," said the stranger. "They will not harm you."

The seal catcher was led into a small cave where a wounded seal lay on a bed of seaweed. It was the seal he had tried to kill that morning.

"He is their king," said the stranger. "He will die unless you take away his pain."

"I will try," said the seal catcher, who was truly sorry now he realized the hurt he had caused. He stretched out his hand to the seal king and gently touched his wound. As he did so, a terrible pain shot through him, making him cry out. Then the pain slowly died away and the seal catcher saw the seal's wound begin to heal. Soon, not even a scar could be seen and the seal king rose from his bed.

Presently the king said to the seal catcher, "You are free to go home now. But first you must promise never to hunt or harm a seal again."

The seal catcher promised, although he knew it would mean giving up his livelihood. The stranger took him up through the dark sea until they were out in the sunlight once more. Then, with one bound, they reached the cliff top. The gray horse was waiting patiently for them and, in no time at all, the seal catcher was returned to his cottage.

The seal catcher became a farmer after that. He threw away his hunting knife and never hunted again, and he enjoyed good fortune to the end of his days.

BILLY BEAR'S STUMPY TAIL

A Scandinavian Tale

One wintry day, Billy Bear met Folly Fox slinking around a frozen pond. Folly Fox was trying to hide a net full of fish that he had just stolen.

"Where did you get such fine fish?" demanded Billy Bear.

"I caught them, of course," replied Folly quickly.

"I would really like to catch some fish," said Billy. "How did you do it?"

Now Folly Fox was jealous of Billy Bear's beautiful bushy tail, so he laughed and said, "It's easy, old friend. You slide onto the ice and cut a hole. Then you dangle your lovely bushy tail down, down into the water, sit on the ice and wait for the fishes to nibble."

Billy Bear wrinkled his nose and pulled a long face.

"Isn't there another way to catch fish?" he growled.

"Not if you want such fine ones as these," said Folly Fox. "Anyway, it's easy. All you have to remember, dear friend, is to keep your tail in the

hole. If you feel a few little nibbles or some pinches now and then, don't take any notice. Just remember that the fish are biting and hanging on to your long tail and that, the longer you wait, the more fish you'll catch!"

Billy Bear growled and grunted suspiciously.

"How do I get the fish out of the water then?" he asked.

"That's easy for a strong bear," chuckled Folly. "First you give a great big push onto your right side then you push yourself over to your left side. Then you stand up quickly and start counting your fishes."

Billy Bear was now convinced.

"My tail is much bigger than yours," he boasted, "so I'm sure to catch twice as many fish as you did."

He lumbered onto the ice, cut out a hole and sat down. Then he wiggled and waggled until his tail was dangling in the water. My, it was cold! But

Billy thought about the wonderful dinner he would soon be having and pushed his tail down deeper into the hole.

Soon his tail was frozen fast in the pond and Billy was shivering with cold.

"Time to go," he chuckled in his growly voice. He rolled over onto his right side. Nothing moved. He pushed hard onto his left side. There was a little creak, creak. Then he heaved himself up with all his strength, just as Folly Fox had told him to.

CRACK!

His tail snapped right off.

Sadly, Billy Bear crawled off the ice. He hadn't caught a single fish and he'd lost his beautiful tail. It never did grow again and that is why, to this day, all bears have stumpy tails.

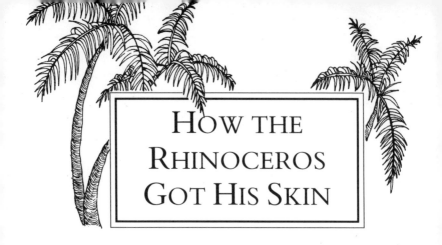

How the Rhinoceros Got His Skin

Rudyard Kipling

Once upon a time, on an uninhabited island on the shores of the Red Sea, there lived a Parsee from whose hat the rays of the sun were reflected in more-than-oriental splendor. And the Parsee lived by the Red Sea with nothing but his hat and his knife and a cooking stove of the kind that you must particularly never touch. And one day he took flour and water and currants and plums and sugar and things, and made himself one cake which was two feet across and three feet thick. It was indeed a Superior Comestible (*that's* Magic), and he put it on the stove because *he* was allowed to cook on that stove, and he baked it and he baked it till it was all done brown and smelled most sentimental.

But just as he was going to eat it there came down to the beach from the Altogether Uninhabited Interior one Rhinoceros with a horn on his nose, two piggy eyes, and few manners. In those days the

Rhinoceros's skin fitted him quite tight. There were no wrinkles in it anywhere. He looked exactly like a Noah's Ark Rhinoceros, but of course much bigger. All the same, he had no manners then, and he has no manners now, and he never will have any manners. He said, "How!" and the Parsee left that cake and climbed to the top of a palm tree with nothing on but his hat, from which the rays of the sun were always reflected, in more-than-oriental splendor. And the Rhinoceros upset the oil stove with his nose, and the cake rolled on the sand, and he spiked that cake on the horn of his nose, and he ate it, and he went away, waving his tail, to the desolate and

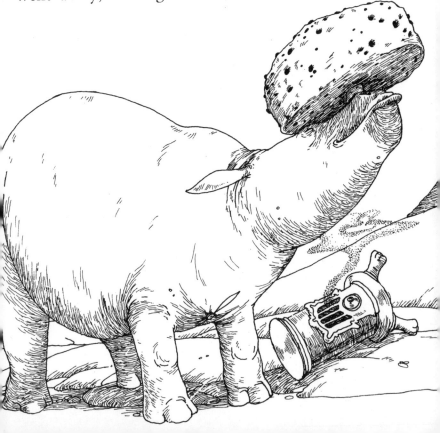

Exclusively Uninhabited Interior which abuts on the islands of Mazanderan, Socotra, and the Promontories of the Larger Equinox. Then the Parsee came down from his palm tree and put the stove on its legs and recited the following *Sloka*, which, as you have not heard, I will now proceed to relate:

"Them that takes cakes
Which the Parsee-man bakes
Makes dreadful mistakes."

And there was a great deal more in that than you would think.

Because, five weeks later, there was a heat wave in the Red Sea, and everybody took off all the clothes they had. The Parsee took off his hat; but the Rhinoceros took off his skin and carried it over his shoulder as he came down to the beach to bathe. In those days it buttoned underneath with three buttons and looked like a raincoat. He said nothing whatever about the Parsee's cake, because he had eaten it all; and he never had any manners, then, since, or henceforward. He waddled straight into the water and blew bubbles through his nose, leaving his skin on the beach.

Presently the Parsee came by and found the skin, and he smiled one smile that ran all around his face two times. Then he danced three times around the skin and rubbed his hands. Then he went to his camp and filled his hat with cake crumbs, for the Parsee

never ate anything but cake, and never swept out his camp. He took that skin, and he shook that skin, and he scrubbed that skin, and he rubbed that skin just as full of old, dry, stale, tickly cake crumbs and some burned currants as ever it could *possibly* hold. Then he climbed to the top of his palm tree and waited for the Rhinoceros to come out of the water and put on his tight-fitting skin.

And the Rhinoceros did. He buttoned it up with the three buttons, and it tickled like cake crumbs in bed. Then he wanted to scratch, but that made it worse; and then he lay down on the sands and rolled and rolled and rolled, and every time he rolled the cake crumbs tickled him worse and worse and worse. Then he ran to the palm tree and rubbed and rubbed and rubbed himself against it. He rubbed so much and so hard that he rubbed his skin into a great fold over his shoulders, and another fold underneath, where the buttons used to be (but he rubbed the buttons off), and he rubbed some more folds over his legs. And it spoiled his temper, but it didn't make the least difference to the cake crumbs. They were inside his skin and they tickled. So he went home, very angry indeed and horribly scratchy; and from that day to this every rhinoceros has great folds in his skin and a very bad temper, all on account of the cake crumbs inside.

But the Parsee came down from his palm tree, wearing his hat, from which the rays of the sun were reflected in more-than-oriental splendor, packed up his cooking stove, and went away in the direction of the Orotavo, the Amygdala, the Upland Meadows of Antananarivo, and the Marshes of Sonaput.

THE THREE BILLY GOATS GRUFF

A Scandinavian Tale

Once upon a time, on the far side of a river, there was a field of rich, green grass. But no animal dared to cross the bridge over the river to eat the grass because a wicked troll with fierce eyes and big teeth lived under the bridge. He hated people and animals and, if anybody tried to cross to the field, he would jump out and gobble them up!

One fine summer's day, the three Billy Goats Gruff looked across the river.

"The grass looks so green over there. Why don't we cross the river and eat some?" they said to one another. So they polished their horns, combed their long, white beards and trotted up to the bridge.

The troll was resting under the bridge when he heard a trip-trap, trip-trap over his head.

"Who is that?" he demanded.

Small Billy Goat Gruff was halfway over the bridge. He called out in his teeny-weeny voice, "It's

only me, Small Billy Goat Gruff."

"You'll make a good dinner," roared the troll. "I'm coming to eat you."

"Oh no!" pleaded Small Billy Goat Gruff. "Don't eat me. My brother, Middle-sized Billy Goat Gruff, will be coming soon. He is much plumper than I am and would make a far better dinner. Why don't you eat him instead?"

"Very well," muttered the troll, and he let Small Billy Goat Gruff go trip-trap across the bridge to the field.

Soon the troll heard the noise of someone walking trip-trap, trip-trap over his head.

"Who is that?" he roarded.

"It's only me, Middle-sized Billy Goat Gruff," said the goat in a middle-sized voice.

"You'll make a good dinner," the troll sneered. "Im coming to eat you."

"Oh no! Don't eat me," said Middle-sized Billy Goat Gruff. "If you let me eat the grass in the field,

I'll be much fatter tomorrow. Why don't you eat Big Billy Goat Gruff today."

"Very well," scowled the troll, and he let Middle-sized Billy Goat Gruff go trip-trap across the bridge. Then he settled down to wait for Big Billy Goat Gruff.

At last he heard a very loud trip-trap, trip-trap coming over the bridge.

"Who is that?" he bellowed.

"It's me, Big Billy Goat Gruff," the goat answered in a big, deep voice.

"You'll make a good dinner," the troll roared. "I'm coming to eat you."

"Oh no, you're not," grinned Big Billy Goat Gruff. "I have sharp, curly horns and I'll toss you into the air."

The troll was furious. He jumped up onto the bridge and rushed at Big Billy Goat Gruff. But Big Billy Goat Gruff was waiting for him. He lowered his head and charged at the troll, and hit him right in the middle with his curly horns.

The troll flew high into the air and fell Splash! into the river. He was carried away by the water and was never ever seen again.

Big Billy Goat Gruff went trip-trap across the bridge to join his two brothers. They munched the rich, green grass happily all day long and soon grew very fat.

THE LIONESS AND THE MOUSE

Aesop

Simba was tired. Of course she was. So would you be if you got up before dawn to hunt breakfast. Especially if breakfast turned out to be very fast on its feet and ran away from you. Simba had chased the zebra for mile after mile across the dusty plain before making the kill. Then she had dragged it all the way back home to her waiting cubs. It was a dog's life being a lioness.

As usual, each cub wanted the lion's share:

"I want leg, I want leg," shouted the first cub.

"You always have it, it's my turn," shrieked the second.

"He's got more than me," yelped the third.

"More, more, more," screamed the fourth.

"S'not fair, s'not fair, s'not fair!" squawked the fifth (she was quite right; s'never fair).

"Oh, shut up," roared Simba. "You're behaving like a lot of spoiled children. Just remember that

80

you're lions. It's all good meat and there's plenty for everybody. So not another murmur."

After that the cubs were as quiet as mice. Which was very sensible because their mother was a lioness, after all, and she had huge paws and razor-sharp claws.

"Right, you lot," growled Simba, as soon as they had finished, "Mommy's going to have a rest and she doesn't want to be disturbed. So run along and play among yourselves. And remember, no squabbling."

She yawned and her cubs could see right inside her cavernous mouth. It was lined with two rows of enormous pointed teeth. You don't argue with teeth like that, thought the little cubs, and off they ran to play.

Simba padded down to the water hole for a long, refreshing drink. Then she settled in the long grass in the shade of a great tree. Peace and quiet at last. Lions just don't realize how much we lionesses have to do, she thought, as she began to doze. It's all very well for lions; they just lie around all day – and all night too, as often as not. Her lion was like that. Just because of his great mane and beard, he thought he was too good to help with the cubs. But she was much too exhausted to bother about all this for long and soon she fell into a deep sleep.

Mouse was tired too. He had spent the night running away from Owl, who had already eaten his mother, father, sister, brother, and his great aunt Squeak. It's a dog's life being a mouse, thought Mouse, as he crept through the long grass into the shade of the great tree. The soft, warm, golden, furry heap he burrowed into was just what he had been looking for.

"The perfect place to lie on," murmured Mouse out loud, as he made himself comfortable. He was just beginning to drift off into sleep when something rough, sharp and very powerful seized him by the throat. Simba was dreaming of a magical world where lions did all the work and the lionesses lay

about sleeping and playing games. It was a delightful dream and she was not at all pleased to be woken up. When she saw what was in her paw she could hardly believe her eyes. A mouse! A tiny little mouse on a great lioness. Mouse was terrified.

"Oh dear," squeaked Mouse, "I'm-m-m-m-m most terribly sorry."

"Sorry!" roared Simba. "Sorry, you sniveling little rodent! I'll make you sorry alright."

She raised her other paw. It would soon be all over for Mouse.

"No, mighty Simba, I beg you, don't do it. It was all a dreadful mousetake."

"Mousetake! Mousetake! Thought I was dead did you? Well listen to me, young man. Even if I were dead and stuffed full of straw in a natural history museum you should show respect – and I mean respect – to me, a great lioness. You've no excuse."

"Oh Simba, Simba," pleaded Mouse, who was ready to try anything, "You're much too important to bother with a wretched little thing like me. In any case, I'm sure I'll taste disgusting."

Simba screwed up her great cat's face.

"Me eat you? Eat a mouse? Ugh! Lionesses don't eat mice, young man. They eat antelope, zebra, and cattle. Besides, I'm not in the least bit hungry. Eat a mouse, ha! What a load of mousetrap, I mean claptrap."

"Oh dear, oh dear, oh dear," said Mouse, more desperate than ever. "Please, please, please don't kill me. Since my life is worth nothing, my death is worth even less. And if I live, who knows, I may be able to help you one day."

Simba roared again, only this time with laughter.

"Ha, ha, ha, ho, ho, ho! You help me?. That's rich. A mouse help a lioness. Now I've heard everything."

She looked at the tiny creature clamped in her paw. There was a twinkle in her smoldering brown eyes.

"Go on then, off you go, before anyone sees us. It

would ruin my reputation if it got around that I'd gone soft on mice."

Mouse scurried off into the undergrowth, grateful for his escape but more exhausted than ever. There's just no future in being a mouse, he thought, wishing he were a hundred times the size, like Simba, for instance.

But big as she was, Simba was in trouble. As Mouse scurried away, a crack of gunshot echoed behind him. Simba leaped up in pain and then fell to the ground. She struggled to get up again but she felt too weak. She had been shot with a tranquilizer. As she lay there, unable to move, a group of men came out of the cover of the trees and threw a net over her. She was trapped. Moments later she fainted. When Simba woke she felt terrible. Her head ached and the net bit into her skin. She couldn't move, and when she tried to roar for help her voice was pitifully weak. Her whole body was sore. They had dragged her a long way.

"It's all over for me," she moaned. "They'll take me somewhere cold and wet and stick me in a smelly little cage. People will bring their children to point at me through the bars. And I'll never see my little cubs again."

Tears sprang into Simba's eyes and rolled down her cheeks.

Mouse was out of breath: "Phew!" he panted. "At last."

He was only a little mouse and already very tired. It had been hard work keeping up with the men.

After a few minutes he got his breath back.

"Right," he squeaked briskly. "There's no time to waste. You just lie there, Simba, and watch this."

He began to gnaw at the net. It was made of special tough rope but Mouse had specially sharp little teeth. He had soon bitten through it in several places, and Simba managed to get her paws through the holes and do the rest. She was very grateful.

"Mouse," she purred, when they were miles away and safe, "I'm very sorry I laughed at you. It just goes to show that size isn't everything. I don't know how to thank you!"

"Don't mention it, mighty Simba, don't mention it. And now, if you don't mind, I'll go to sleep again."

Mouse burrowed deeper into the soft, warm, golden, furry heap without a care in the world. Perhaps it wasn't so bad being a mouse after all.

HOW THE POLAR BEAR BECAME

Ted Hughes

When the animals had been on earth for some time they grew tired of admiring the trees, the flowers, and the sun. They began to admire each other. Every animal was eager to be admired, and spent a part of each day making itself look more beautiful.

Soon they began to hold beauty contests.

Sometimes Tiger won the prize, sometimes Eagle, and sometimes Ladybug. Every animal tried hard.

One animal in particular won the prize almost every time. This was Polar Bear.

Polar Bear was white. Not quite snowy white, but much whiter than any of the other creatures. Everyone admired her. In secret, too, everyone was envious of her. But however much they wished that she wasn't quite so beautiful, they couldn't help giving her the prize.

"Polar Bear," they said, "with your white fur, you are almost too beautiful."

All this went to Polar Bear's head. In fact, she became vain. She was always washing and polishing her fur, trying to make it still whiter. After a while she was winning the prize every time. The only times any other creature got a chance to win was when it rained. On those days Polar Bear would say:

"I shall not go out into the wet. The other creatures will be muddy and my white fur may get splashed."

Then, perhaps, Frog or Duck would win for a change.

She had a crowd of young admirers who were always hanging around her cave. They were mainly Seals, all very giddy. Whenever she came out they made a loud shrieking roar:

"Ooooooh! How beautiful she is!"

Before long, her white fur was more important to Polar Bear than anything. Whenever a single speck of dust landed on the tip of one hair of it – she was furious.

"How can I be expected to keep beautiful in this country!" she cried then. "None of you have ever seen me at my best because of the dirt here. I am really much whiter than any of you have ever seen me. I think I shall have to go into another country. A country where there is none of this dust. Which country would be best?"

She used to talk this way because then the Seals would cry:

"Oh, please don't leave us. Please don't take your beauty away from us. We will do anything for you."

And she loved to hear this.

Soon animals were coming from all over the world to look at her. They stared and stared as Polar Bear stretched out on her rock in the sun. Then they went off home and tried to make themselves look like her. But it was no use. They were all the wrong color. They were black, or brown, or yellow, or ginger, or fawn, or speckled, but none of them was white. Soon most of them gave up trying to look beautiful. But they still came every day to gaze enviously at Polar Bear. Some brought picnics. They sat in a vast crowd among the trees in front of her cave.

"Just look at her," said Mother Hippo to her children. "Now see that you grow up like that."

But nothing pleased Polar Bear.

"The dust these crowds raise!" she sighed. "Why can't I ever get away from them? If only there were some spotless, shining country, all for me . . ."

Now pretty well all the creatures were tired of her being so much more admired than they were. But one creature more so than the rest. He was Peregrine Falcon.

He was a beautiful bird, all right. But he was not white. Time and time again, in the beauty contest he was runner-up to Polar Bear.

"If it were not for her," he raged to himself, "I should be first every time."

He thought and thought of a plan to get rid of her. How? How? How? At last he had it.
One day he went up to Polar Bear.

Now Peregrine Falcon had been to every country in the world. He was a great traveler, as all the creatures well knew.

"I know a country," he said to Polar Bear, "which is so clean it is even whiter then you are. Yes, yes, I know, you are beautifully white, but this country is even whiter. The rocks are clean glass and the earth is frozen ice cream. There is no dirt there, no dust, no mud. You would become whiter than ever in that country. And no one lives there. You could be queen of it."

Polar Bear tried to hide her excitement.

"I could be queen of it, you say?" she cried. "This country sounds made for me. No crowds, no dirt? And the rocks, you say, are glass?"

"The rocks," said Peregrine Falcon, "are mirrors."

"Wonderful," said Polar Bear.

"And the rain," he said, "is white face powder."

"Better than ever!" she cried. "How quickly can I be there, away from all these staring crowds and all this dirt?"

"I am going to another country," she told the other animals. "It is too dirty here to live."

Peregrine Falcon hired Whale to carry his passenger. He sat on Whale's forehead, calling out the

directions. Polar Bear sat on the shoulder, gazing at the sea. The Seals, who had begged to go with her, sat on the tail.

After some days, they came to the North Pole, where it is all snow and ice.

"Here you are," cried Peregrine Falcon. "Everything just as I said. No crowds, no dirt, nothing but beautiful clean whiteness."

"And the rocks actually are mirrors!" cried Polar Bear, and she ran to the nearest iceberg to repair her beauty after the long trip.

Every day now, she sat on one iceberg or another, making herself beautiful in the mirror of ice. Always, near her, sat the Seals. Her fur became whiter and whiter in this new clean country. And as it became whiter, the Seals praised her beauty more

and more. When she herself saw the improvement
in her looks she said:

"I shall never go back to that dirty old country
again."

And there she still is, with all her admirers around
her.

Peregrine Falcon flew back to the other creatures
and told them that Polar Bear had gone for ever.
They were all very glad, and set about making
themselves beautiful at once. Every single one was
saying to himself:

"Now that Polar Bear is out of the way, perhaps I
shall have a chance of the prize at the beauty
contest."

And Peregrine Falcon was saying to himself:

"Surely, now, I am the most beautiful of all
creatures."

But that first contest was won by a Little Brown
Mouse for her pink feet.

HENNY PENNY

An English Tale

In a field on a farm there grew a big chestnut tree. One day, a chicken called Chicky-Licky was sleeping under this tree when suddenly a prickly chestnut fell, plop, onto her head.

"Oh my, the sky is falling down!" she exclaimed. "I'd better run and tell everyone about it." So she ran and ran until she met a speckledy hen.

"Henny-Penny," cried Chicky-Licky, quite out of breath, "the sky is falling down. A piece fell on me."

"We must tell the king about this," said Henny-Penny. So off they ran until they met Ducky-Lucky.

"Ducky-Lucky," clucked Henny-Penny, "the sky is falling down. A piece just fell on Chicky-Licky and we're going to tell the king about it."

"I'll come with you," quacked Ducky-Lucky. So

the three birds ran and ran until they met Goosey-Loosey.

"Goosey-Loosey," clucked Henny-Penny, "the sky is falling down. A big piece fell on Chicky-Licky and we're off to tell the king."

"I'm coming too," screeched Goosey-Loosey. So the four birds ran and ran until they met Turkey-Lurkey.

"Turkey-Lurkey," cried Henny-Penny, "have your heard the news? The sky is falling down and a great big piece fell on Chicky-Licky. We're on our way to tell the king all about it."

"I'm coming too," gobbled Turkey-Lurkey. So the five birds ran and ran until they met Foxy-Loxy.

"Foxy-Loxy," clucked Henny-Penny, "the sky is falling down. An enormous piece fell on Chicky-Licky and we are on our way to tell the king about it."

"Well, well, well," said Foxy-Loxy. "His Majesty will be most interested. Do you know where he lives?"

"Certainly," replied Henny-Penny. "He lives in a castle with a golden roof and diamonds in the windows."

"I'm afraid you are wrong, Henny-Penny," said Foxy-Loxy. "He lives in a palace under the hill. His Majesty often asks me to visit him, so I know the way very well."

"Please could you show us the way then?" cried the five birds together, flapping their wings excitedly.

"It will be a pleasure," grinned Foxy-Loxy, trying to hide his large teeth under his ginger whiskers. "It isn't very far from here at all. Just keep close behind me and I will lead you straight there!"

So Chicky-Licky and Henny-Penny and Ducky-Lucky and Goosey-Loosey and Turkey-Lurkey and Foxy-Loxy ran and ran until they came to a deep hole in the hillside.

"Keep close to me," said Foxy-Loxy. So they all followed Foxy-Loxy down the hole and into the hillside.

And, sad to say, that was the end of Chicky-Licky and Ducky-Lucky and Goosey-Loosey and Turkey-Lurkey. Henny-Penny was the last to enter Foxy-Loxy's hole, and she heard Chicky-Licky crowing with alarm in front of her. Squawking with fright, she turned and ran as fast as she could for the safety of the farm. There she stayed, and she never did tell the king that the sky was falling down.

The Ostrich and The Hedgehog

An African Tale

One beautiful summer's morning, a hedgehog set off for a walk across the sandy desert. He was going to see how far the barley had grown in a nearby barley field. The hedgehog had watched the barley grow from the first tiny, green shoots. Now the stalks were so tall that they towered above his head and the barley would soon be ready for harvesting.

"There's no finer sight than a field of golden barley in the desert," the hedgehog said contentedly.

As he stood on the edge of the field admiring the view, a great gawky ostrich came striding along. Now ostriches cannot fly, so they have to walk or run everywhere on their strong legs. But they can certainly run very fast.

The hedgehog looked up at the ostrich and called out, "Good morning," in a cheery voice.

But the ostrich merely looked down his nose at

the hedgehog and said in a superior voice, "I am not in the habit of talking to stumpy-legged creatures like you."

"My legs may be stumpy," replied the hedgehog, bristling indignantly, "but, I can run faster on them than any other animal for miles around."

"Humph!" scoffed the ostrich. "No one can run faster than I can, with my strong, long legs."

The hedgehog's eyes twinkled.

"That's what you think," he said. "Why don't we have a race? Then we'll see who is the faster runner – you or I."

"Oh, it's sure to be me!" boasted the ostrich. "Let's race now, shall we? On the count of three. One, two . . ."

"Wait a minute," said the hedgehog. "I haven't had my breakfast yet. I can't run on an empty

stomach! We'll meet back here at midday. Then we'll race each other up and down between the rows of barley. Is that agreed?"

The ostrich nodded, thinking that nothing could be easier than racing against such a dumpy little creature. He went off to take a nap, burying his head in the sand as ostriches do.

As soon as the ostrich had gone, the hedgehog raced back home as fast as he could, calling to his family, "Please come quickly, all of you! There's something I want you to do for me in the barley field."

So all the hedgehog's family — mother and father, brothers, sisters, cousins, even aunts and uncles – ran up to the barley field and gathered around him. There he explained to them what he wanted.

"You must help me win a race against the ostrich," he said.

"But how?" asked the other hedgehogs. "You can't hope to beat the ostrich, with his great, long legs."

"I can and I will, if you all listen carefully and do as I ask," replied the hedgehog. "You must all go and position yourselves so that there is one of you at the end of each row of barley. The ostrich and I will start the race at the beginning of the first row, but when he is a few yards ahead of me, I shall turn back. Now, when the ostrich comes racing up to the end of the row, one of you will be sitting there, pretending to be a bit out of breath from running so fast. He will think it is me. Then, when he reaches the end of the next row and sees another hedgehog a bit out of breath, he will think I've beaten him again. And so on."

The hedgehogs thought this was a brilliant idea and they quickly ran off to take up their positions.

At midday, the ostrich returned to the barley field. He was refreshed from his sleep and looked very smug at the thought of winning the race. He lined up with the hedgehog at the start of the first row of barley.

"Are you ready?" he asked.

The hedgehog nodded.

"Then one, two, three – GO!" shouted the ostrich, and off he ran with great strides, smirking to himself and leaving the hedgehog far behind. But when the ostrich reached the end of the first barley row, what did he see? The hedgehog was already there, puffing and panting and calling to him, "Ah, there you are at last."

The ostrich was so surprised he did not reply. Off he ran, even faster, along the next row, but when he came to the end, what did he see? The hedgehog, standing waiting, a little out of breath, but calling, "You've arrived at last."

Again and again the ostrich raced away, running as he had never run before. But each time he reached the end of a row, what did he see? A hedgehog! The

ostrich could not tell the difference between one
hedgehog and another, so he did not realize that he
had seen several hedgehogs – not just one. When he
reached the end of the last row, panting and
completely exhausted, what did he see? A hedgehog, looking as fresh as a daisy and calling, "So
you've made it at last!"

The ostrich could not understand how he had been beaten by a stumpy little hedgehog. He limped off on his tired, sore feet and buried his head deep in the sand. He was so embarrassed at losing the race that he didn't show his face again for a very, very long time.

THE TWO FROGS

A Japanese Tale

Many years ago there were two frogs who lived in faraway Japan. A cosy ditch in a seaside town called Osaka was home for one while the other lived in a stream which trickled through Kyoto. They were happy frogs. Then, curiously, at the same time they had the same idea. They decided to travel and look at the rest of the world.

"I'd like to see the Mikado's wonderful palace in Kyoto." croaked one.

"I've never seen the sea at Osaka," honked the other.

So early one morning both frogs set off. They traveled along the same road but one started from Osaka and the other from Kyoto. The road was long and dusty. Their legs grew tired and they had to leap into deep grass many times to rest and cool off. About halfway, each noticed a high mountain which they had to climb. Hop, hop they went, getting slower and slower until they reached the top. Croaking happily, both jumped into a cooling pond and almost crashed head on!

"I'm sorry," the first frog said politely, "I wasn't expecting company."

"Neither was I," said the other. "This is a pleasant surprise." Both washed off the dust, then they hopped over to some cool damp shade under a stone and stretched out their weary legs.

"I've heard Kyoto has many wonderful palaces," began the first frog, "I'd like to see them and the rest of Japan too."

"I've never seen a ship and I'd love to see the beach and a whale and perhaps a shark," replied the second one.

"I don't care for whales or sharks," the first frog shuddered. "They're rather big, you see. Have you ever seen the Mikado?"

"N-o-o, not exactly," was the reply, "but I've seen his soldiers." They chatted about their homes and agreed that it was difficult to keep cool in the summer in either Osaka or Kyoto.

"This mountain is halfway between both towns," said the Osaka frog. "It's so high that if we were taller we could see both places at once. Then we could decide whether we wanted to go on."

"What a good idea," replied the Kyoto frog. "I'll tell you what we'll do. We'll stand on our back legs and hold each other up, then we'll get a good view at the same time.

Both frogs jumped up. They stretched as high as they could on their back legs and clutched each other very tightly. The Kyoto frog looked over his new friend's shoulder toward Osaka. The Osaka frog looked over his friend's shoulder to Kyoto. But those silly frogs forgot that when they were standing up, their eyes were at the back of their head. You can check for yourself!

"Dear, dear, Kyoto is exactly like Osaka," cried one, "What a waste of time my journey has been!"

"Osaka is the same as Kyoto," exclaimed the other. "I may as well have stayed at home!"

They dropped their front legs and down they fell, *ker-plot*. Both frogs bowed politely to each other and hopped back home.

The towns of Osaka and Kyoto are as different as chalk and cheese, but for the rest of their lives those frogs believed they were exactly the same. They never wanted to leave their comfortable damp little homes again – ever!

TIGERS FOREVER

Ruskin Bond

On the left bank of the Ganges River, where it flows out from the Himalayan foothills, is a long stretch of heavy forest. There are villages on the fringe of the forest, inhabited by farmers and herdsmen. Big game hunters came to the area for many years, and as a result the animals had been getting fewer. The trees, too, had been disappearing slowly; and as the animals lost their food and shelter, they moved farther into the foothills.

There was a time when this forest had provided a home for some thirty to forty tigers, but men in search of skins and trophies had shot them all, and now there remained only one old tiger in the jungle. The hunters had tried to get him too, but he was a wise and crafty tiger, who knew the ways of man, and so far he had survived all attempts on his life.

Although the tiger had passed the prime of his life, he had lost none of his majesty. His muscles rippled beneath the golden yellow of his coat, and he walked through the long grass with the confidence of one who knew that he was still a king, although his subjects were fewer. His great head pushed through the foliage, and it was only his tail, swinging high, that sometimes showed above the sea of grass.

He was heading for water, the water of a large marsh, where he sometimes went to drink or cool off. The marsh was usually deserted except when the buffaloes from a nearby village were brought there to bathe or wallow in the muddy water.

The tiger waited in the shelter of a rock, his ears pricked for any unfamiliar sound. He knew that it was here that hunters sometimes waited for him with guns.

He walked into the water, in among the water lilies, and drank slowly. He was seldom in a hurry while he ate and drank.

He raised his head and listened, one paw suspended in the air.

A strange sound had come to him on the breeze, and he was wary of strange sounds. So he moved swiftly into the shelter of the tall grass that bordered the marsh, and climbed a hillock until he reached his favorite rock. This rock was big enough to hide him and give him shade.

The sound he had heard was only a flute, sounding thin and reedy in the forest. It belonged to Nandu, a slim brown boy who rode a buffalo.

Nandu played vigorously on the flute. Chottu, a slightly smaller boy, riding another buffalo, brought up the rear of the herd.

There were eight buffaloes in the herd, which belonged to the families of Nandu and Chottu, who were cousins. Their fathers sold buffalo-milk and butter in villages farther down the river.

The tiger had often seen them at the marsh, and he was not bothered by their presence. He knew the village folk would leave him alone as long as he did not attack their buffaloes. And as long as there were deer in the jungle, he would not be interested in other prey.

He decided to move on and find a cool, shady place in the heart of the jungle, where he could rest during the hot afternoon and be free of the flies and mosquitoes that swarmed around the marsh. At night he would hunt.

With a lazy grunt that was half a roar, "A-oonh!" – he got off his haunches and sauntered off into the jungle.

The gentlest of tigers' roars can be heard a mile away, and the boys, who were barely fifty yards distant, looked up immediately.

"There he goes!" said Nandu, taking the flute from his lips and pointing with it toward the hillock. "Did you see him?"

"I saw his tail, just before he disappeared. He's a big tiger!"

"Don't call him tiger. Call him Uncle."

"Why?" asked Chottu.

"Because it's unlucky to call a tiger a tiger. My father told me so. But if you call him Uncle, he will leave you alone."

"I see," said Chottu. "You have to make him a relative. I'll try and remember that."

The buffaloes were now well into the marsh, and some of them were lying down in the mud. Buffaloes love soft wet mud and will wallow in it for hours. Nandu and Chottu were not so fond of the mud, so they went swimming in deeper water. Later, they rested in the shade of an old silk-cotton tree.

At dawn next day Chottu was in the jungle on his own, gathering mahua flowers. The flowers of the mahua tree can be eaten by animals as well as humans. Chottu's mother made them into a jam, of which he was particularly fond. Bears like them, too, and will eat them straight off the tree.

Chottu climbed a large mahua tree – leafless when in bloom – and began breaking the white flowers and throwing them to the ground. He had been in the tree for about five minutes when he heard the sound made by a bear – a sort of whining grumble – and presently a young bear ambled into the clearing beneath the tree.

115

It was a small bear, little more than a cub, and Chottu was not frightened. But he knew the mother bear might be close by, so he decided to take no chances and sat very still, waiting to see what the bear would do. He hoped it wouldn't choose the same tree for a breakfast of mahua flowers.

At first the young bear put his nose to the ground and sniffed his way along until he came to a large ant hill. Here he began huffing and puffing, blowing rapidly in and out of his nose, making the dust from the ant hill fly in all directions. Bears love eating ants! But he was a disappointed bear, because the ant hill had been deserted long ago. And so, grumbling, he made his way across to a wild plum tree. Shinning rapidly up the smooth trunk, he was soon perched in the upper branches. It was only then he saw Chottu.

The bear at once scrambled several feet higher up the tree – the wild plum grows quite tall – and laid himself out flat on a branch. It wasn't a very thick branch and left a large expanse of bear showing on either side. He tucked his head away behind another branch and, so long as he could not see the boy, seemed quite satisfied that he was well hidden, though he couldn't help grumbling with anxiety. Like most animals, he could smell humans, and he was afraid of them.

Bears, however, are also very curious. And slowly, inch by inch, the young bear's black snout appeared over the edge of the branch. Immediately he saw Chottu, he drew back with a jerk and his head was once more hidden.

The bear did this two or three times, and Chottu, now greatly amused, waited until it wasn't looking, then moved some way down the tree. When the bear looked up again and saw that the boy was missing, he was so pleased with himself that he stretched right across to the next branch, to get a plum. Chottu chose this moment to burst into laughter.

The startled bear tumbled out of the tree, dropped through the branches for a distance of some fifteen feet, and landed with a thud in a heap of dry leaves.

And then several things happened at almost the same time.

The mother bear came charging into the clearing. Spotting Chottu, she reared up on her hind legs, grunting fiercely.

It was Chottu's turn to be startled. There are few animals more dangerous than a rampaging mother bear, and the boy knew that one blow from her clawed forepaws could finish him.

But before the bear reached the tree, there was a tremendous roar, and the tiger bounded into the clearing. He had been asleep in the bushes not far away, having feasted well on a spotted deer the previous night. He liked a good sleep after a heavy meal, and now the noise in the clearing had woken him, putting him in a very bad mood.

The tiger's roar made his displeasure quite clear. Both bears turned and ran away from the clearing, the younger one squealing with fright.

The tiger then came into the clearing, looked up at the trembling boy, and roared again.

Chottu nearly fell out of the tree.

"Good day to you, Uncle," he stammered, showing his teeth in a nervous grin.

Perhaps this was too much for the tiger. With a low growl, he turned his back on the mahua tree and padded off into the jungle, his tail twitching in disgust.

The following evening, when Nandu and Chottu came home with the buffalo herd, they found a crowd of curious villagers surrounding a jeep in which sat three strangers with guns. They were hunters, and they were accompanied by servants and a large store of provisions.

They had heard that there was a tiger in the area, and they wanted to shoot it.

These men had money to spend; and, as most of the villagers were poor, they were prepared to go into the forest to make a tree-platform for the hunters. The platform, big enough to take the three men, was put up in the branches of a tall mahogany tree.

Nandu was told by his father to tie a goat at the foot of the tree. While these preparations were being made, Chottu slipped off and circled the area, with a plan of his own in mind. He had no wish to see the tiger killed – he felt he owed it a favor for saving him from the bear – and he had decided to give it some sort of warning. So he tied up bits and pieces of old clothing on small trees and bushes. He knew the wily old king of the jungle would keep well away from the area if he saw the bits of clothing – for where there were men's clothes, there would be men.

The vigil kept by the hunters lasted all through the night, but the tiger did not come near the tree. Perhaps he'd got Chottu's warning; or perhaps he wasn't hungry.

It was a cold night, and it wasn't long before the hunters opened their flasks of rum. Soon they were whispering among themselves; then they were chattering so loudly that no wild animal would have come near them. By morning they were fast asleep.

They looked grumpy and shamefaced as they trudged back to the village.

"Wrong time of year for tiger," said the first hunter.

"Nothing left in these parts," said the second.

"I think I've caught a cold," said the third.

And they drove away in disgust.

It was not until the beginning of the summer that something happened to alter the hunting habits of the tiger and bring him into conflict with the villagers.

There had been no rain for almost two months, and the tall jungle grass had become a sea of billowy dry yellow. Some city-dwellers, camping near the forest, had been careless while cooking and had started a forest fire. Slowly it spread into the interior, from where the acrid fumes smoked the tiger out toward the edge of the jungle. As night came on, the flames grew more vivid, the smell stronger. The tiger turned and made for the marsh, where he knew he would be safe provided he swam across to the little island in the center.

Next morning he was on the island, which was untouched by the fire. But his surroundings had changed. The slope of the hills were black with burned grass, and most of the tall bamboo had disappeared. The deer and the wild pig, finding that their natural cover had gone, moved farther east.

When the fire had died down and the smoke had cleared, the tiger prowled through the forest again but found no game. He drank at the marsh and settled down in a shady spot to sleep.

The tiger spent four days looking for game. By that time he was so hungry that he even resorted to rooting among the dead leaves and burned stumps of trees, searching for worms and beetles. This was a sad comedown for the king of the jungle. But even now he hesitated to leave the area in search of new hunting grounds, for he had a deep fear and

suspicion of the forests farther east – forests that were fast being swept away by human habitation. He could have gone north, into the high mountains, but they did not provide him with the long grass he needed for cover.

At break of day he came to the marsh. The water was now shallow and muddy, and a green scum had spread over the top. He drank, and then lay down across his favorite rock, hoping for a deer; but none came. He was about to get up and lope away when he heard an animal approach.

The tiger at once slipped off his rock and flattened himself on the ground, his tawny stripes merging with the dry grass.

A buffalo emerged from the jungle and came to the water.

The buffalo was alone.

He was a big male, and his long curved horns lay right across his shoulders. He moved leisurely toward the water, completely unaware of the tiger's presence.

The tiger hesitated before making his charge.

It was a long time – many years – since he had killed a buffalo, and he knew instinctively that the villagers would be angry. But the pangs of hunger overcame his caution. There was no morning breeze, everything was still, and the smell of the tiger did not reach the buffalo. A monkey chattered on a nearby tree, but his warning went unheeded.

Crawling stealthily on his stomach, the tiger skirted the edge of the marsh and approached the buffalo from behind. The buffalo was standing in shallow water, drinking, when the tiger charged from the side and sank his teeth into his victim's thigh.

The buffalo staggered, but turned to fight. He snorted and lowered his horns at the tiger. But the cat was too fast for the brave buffalo. He bit into the other leg and the buffalo crashed to the ground. Then the tiger moved in for the kill.

After resting, he began to eat. Although he had been starving for days, he could not finish the huge carcass. And so he quenched his thirst at the marsh and dragged the remains of the buffalo into the bushes, to conceal it from jackals and vultures; then he went off to find a place to sleep.

He would return to the kill when he was hungry.

The herdsmen were naturally very upset when they discovered that a buffalo was missing. And next day, when Nandu and Chottu came running home to say that they had found the half-eaten carcass near the marsh, the men of the village grew angry. They knew that once the tiger realized how easy it was to kill their animals, he would make a habit of it.

Kundan Singh, Nandu's father, who owned the buffalo, said he would go after the tiger himself.

"It's too late now," said his wife. "You should never have let the buffalo roam on its own."

"He had been on his own before. This is the first time the tiger has attacked one of our animals."

"He must have been very hungry," said Chottu.

"Well, we are hungry too," said Kundan Singh. "Our best buffalo – the only male in the herd. It will cost me at least two thousand rupees to buy another."

"The tiger will kill again," said Chottu's father. "Many years ago a tiger did the same thing. He became a cattle-killer."

"Should we send for the hunters?"

"No, they are clumsy fools. We will have to shoot him ourselves. Tonight he will return to the carcass for another meal. You have a gun?"

Kundan Singh smiled proudly and, going to a cupboard, brought out a double-barreled gun. It looked ancient!

"My father bought it from an Englishman," he said.

"How long ago was that?"

"About the time I was born."

"And have you ever used it?" asked Chottu's father, looking at the old gun with distrust.

"A few years ago I let it off at some bandits. Don't

you remember? When I fired, they did not stop running until they had crossed the river.''

"Yes, but did you hit anyone?''

"I would have, if someone's goat hadn't gotten in the way.''

"We had roast meat that night,'' said Nandu.

Accompanied by Chottu's father and several others, Kundan set out for the marsh, where, without shifting the buffalo's carcass – for they knew the tiger would not come near them if he suspected a trap – they made another tree-platform in the branches of a tall tree some thirty feet from the kill.

Late that evening, Kundan Singh and Chottu's father settled down for the night on their rough platform.

Several hours passed and nothing but a jackal was seen by the watchers. And then, just as the moon came up over the distant hills, the two men were

startled by a low "A-oonh," followed by a suppressed grumbling
growl.

Kundan tightened his grip on
the old gun. There was complete
silence for a minute or two, then
the sound of stealthy footfalls.

A moment later the tiger
walked out into the moonlight and
stood over his kill.

At first Kundan could do nothing. He was completely taken
aback by the size of the tiger.
Chottu's father had to nudge him,
and then Kundan quickly put the
gun to his shoulder, aimed at the
tiger's head, and pressed
the trigger.

The gun went off with a flash and two loud bangs, as Kundan fired both barrels. There was a tremendous roar. The tiger rushed at the tree and tried to leap into the branches. Fortunately the platform was at a good height, and the tiger was unable to reach it.

He roared again and then bounded off into the forest.

"What a tiger!" exclaimed Kundan, half in fear and half in admiration.

"You missed him completely," said Chottu's father.

"I did not," said Kundan. "You heard him roar! Would he have been so angry if he had not been hit?"

"Well, if you have only wounded him, he will turn into a man-eater – and where will that leave us?"

"He won't be back," said Kundan. "He will leave this area."

During the next few days the tiger lay low. He did not go near the marsh except when it was very dark and he was very thirsty. The herdsmen and villagers decided that the tiger had gone away. Nandu and Chottu – usually accompanied by other village youths, and always carrying their small hand-axes – began bringing the buffaloes to the marsh again during the day; they were careful not to let any of them stray far from the herd.

But one day, while the boys were taking the herd

home, one of the buffaloes lagged behind.

Nandu did not realize that an animal was missing until he heard an agonized bellow behind him. He glanced over his shoulder just in time to see the tiger dragging the buffalo into a clump of bamboo. The herd sensed the danger, and the buffaloes snorted with fear as they hurried along the forest path. To urge them forward and to warn his friends, Nandu cupped his hands to his mouth and gave a yodeling call.

The buffaloes bellowed, the boys shouted, and the birds flew shrieking from the trees. Together they stampeded out of the forest. The villagers heard the thunder of hoofs, and saw the herd coming home amid clouds of dust.

131

"The tiger!" called Nandu. "He's taken another buffalo!"

He is afraid of us no longer, thought Chottu. And now everyone will hate him and do their best to kill him.

"Did you see where he went?" asked Kundan. "I will take my gun and a few men, and wait near the bridge. The rest of you must beat the jungle from this side and drive the tiger toward me. He will not escape this time, unless he swims the river!"

Kundan took his men and headed for the suspension bridge across the river, while the others, guided by Nandu and Chottu, went to the spot where the tiger had seized the buffalo.

The tiger was still eating when he heard the men coming. He had not expected to be disturbed so soon. With an angry "Woof!" he bounded into the jungle, and watched the men – there were some twenty of them – through a screen of leaves and tall grass.

The men carried hand drums slung from their shoulders, and some carried sticks and spears. After a hurried consultation, they strung out in a line and entered the jungle beating their drums.

The tiger did not like the noise. He went deeper into the jungle. But the men came after him, banging away on their drums and shouting at the tops of their voices. They advanced singly or in pairs, but nowhere were they more than fifteen yards apart.

The tiger could easily have broken through this slowly advancing semicircle of men – one swift blow from his paw would have felled the strongest of them – but his main object was to get away from the noise. He hated the noise made by men.

He was not a man-eater and he would not attack a man unless he was very angry or very frightened; and as yet he was neither. He had eaten well, and he would have liked to rest – but there would be no chance of rest for him until the men ceased their tremendous clatter and din.

Nandu and Chottu kept close to their elders, knowing it wouldn't be safe to go back on their own. Chottu felt sorry for the tiger; he hadn't forgotten the day when the tiger had saved him from the bear.

"Do they have to kill the tiger?" he asked. "If they drive him across the river he won't come back, will he?"

"Why not?" said Nandu. "He's found it easy to kill our buffaloes, and when he's hungry he'll come again. We have to live too."

Chottu was silent. He could see no way out for the tiger.

For an hour the villagers beat the jungle, shouting, drumming, and trampling the undergrowth.

The tiger had no rest. Whenever he was able to put some distance between himself and the men, he would sink down in some shady spot to rest; but, within a few minutes, the trampling and drumming would come nearer, and with an angry snarl he would get up again and pad northward, along the narrowing strip of jungle, toward the bridge across the river.

It was about noon when the tiger finally came into the open. The boys had a clear view of him as he moved slowly along, now in the open, now in the shade or passing through the shorter grass. He was still out of range of Kundan Singh's gun, but there was no way in which he could retreat.

He disappeared among some bushes but soon reappeared to retrace his steps. The beaters had done their work well. The tiger was now only about a hundred and fifty yards from the place where Kundan Singh waited.

The beat had closed in, the men were now bunched together. They were making a great noise, but nothing moved.

Chottu, watching from a distance, wondered: Has he slipped through the beaters? And in his heart he hoped so.

Tins clashed, drums beat, and some of the men poked into the reeds along the river bank with their spears or bamboo sticks. Perhaps one of these thrusts found its mark, because at last the tiger was roused, and with an angry, desperate snarl he charged out of the reeds, splashing through an inlet of mud and water.

Kundan Singh fired and missed.

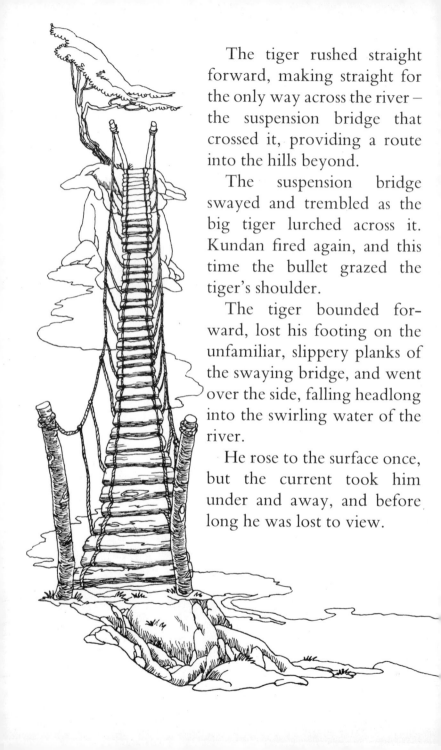

The tiger rushed straight forward, making straight for the only way across the river – the suspension bridge that crossed it, providing a route into the hills beyond.

The suspension bridge swayed and trembled as the big tiger lurched across it. Kundan fired again, and this time the bullet grazed the tiger's shoulder.

The tiger bounded forward, lost his footing on the unfamiliar, slippery planks of the swaying bridge, and went over the side, falling headlong into the swirling water of the river.

He rose to the surface once, but the current took him under and away, and before long he was lost to view.

At first the villagers were glad – they felt their buffaloes were safe. Then they began to feel that something had gone out of their lives, out of the life of the forest. The forest had been shrinking year by year, as more people had moved into the area; but as long as the tiger had been there and they had heard him roar at night, they had known there was still some distance between them and the ever-spreading towns and cities. Now that the tiger had gone, it was as though a protector had gone.

The river had carried the tiger many miles away from his old home, from the forest he had always known, and brought him ashore on the opposite bank of the river, on a strip of warm yellow sand. He lay quite still in the sun, breathing slowly, more soaked than hurt.

Slowly he heaved himself off the ground and moved at a crouch to where tall grass waved in the afternoon breeze. Would he be hunted again, and shot at? There was no smell of man. The tiger moved forward with greater confidence.

There was, however, another smell in the air, a smell that reached back to the time when he was

young and fresh and full of vigor; a smell that he had almost forgotten but could never really forget – the smell of a tigress.

He lifted his head, and new life surged through his limbs. He gave a deep roar, "A-oonh!" and moved purposefully through the tall grass. And the roar came back to him, calling him, urging him forward; a roar that meant there would be more tigers in the land!

That night, half asleep on his cot, Chottu heard the tigers roaring to each other across the river, and he recognized the roar of his own tiger. And from the vigor of its roar he knew that he was alive and safe, and he was glad.

"Let there be tigers forever," he whispered into the darkness before he fell asleep.

TITTY MOUSE
AND
TATTY MOUSE

An English Tale

Titty Mouse and Tatty Mouse both lived in a house. Titty Mouse went gathering corn and Tatty Mouse went gathering corn, so they both went gathering corn. Titty Mouse gathered an ear of corn and Tatty Mouse gathered an ear of corn, so they both gathered an ear of corn.

Titty Mouse made a pudding, and Tatty Mouse made a pudding, so they both made a pudding. And Tatty Mouse put her pudding into the pot to boil, but when Titty went to put hers in, the pot tumbled over, and scalded her to death.

Then Tatty Mouse sat down and wept. A three-legged stool said, "Tatty, why do you weep?"

"Titty's dead," said Tatty, "and so I weep."

"Then," said the stool, "I'll hop." So the stool hopped.

Then a broom in the corner of the room said, "Stool, why do you hop?"

"Oh!" said the stool, "Titty's dead, and Tatty weeps, so I hop."

"Then," said the broom, "I'll sweep." So the broom began to sweep.

Then said the door, "Broom, why do you sweep?"

"Oh!" said the broom, "Titty's dead, and Tatty weeps, and the stool hops, and so I sweep."

"Then," said the door, "I'll jar." So the door jarred.

Then said the window, "Door, why do you jar?"

"Oh!" said the door, "Titty's dead, and Tatty weeps, and the stool hops, and the broom sweeps, and so I jar."

"Then," said the window, "I'll creak." So the window creaked.

Now there was an old bench outside the house, and when the window creaked, the bench said, "Window, why do you creak?"

"Oh!" said the window, "Titty's dead, and Tatty weeps, and the stool hops, and the broom sweeps, the door jars, and so I creak."

"Then," said the bench, "I'll run around the house." So the old bench ran around the house.

Now there was a fine large walnut tree growing by the cottage, and the tree said to the bench, "Bench, why do you run around the house?"

"Oh!" said the bench, "Titty's dead, and Tatty weeps, and the stool hops, and the broom sweeps, the door jars, and the window creaks, and so I run around the house."

"Then," said the walnut tree, "I'll shed my leaves." So the walnut tree shed all its beautiful leaves.

Now there was a little bird perched on one of the boughs of the tree, and when all the leaves fell, it said, "Walnut tree, why do you shed your leaves?"

"Oh!" said the tree, "Titty's dead, and Tatty weeps, the stool hops, and the broom sweeps, the door jars, and the window creaks, the old bench runs around the house, and so I shed my leaves."

"Then," said the little bird, "I'll molt all my feathers." So he molted all his pretty feathers.

Now there was a little girl walking below, carrying a jug of milk for her brothers' and sisters' supper, and when she saw the poor little bird molt all his feathers, she said, "Little bird, why do you molt all your feathers?"

"Oh!" said the little bird, "Titty's dead, and Tatty weeps, the stool hops, and the broom sweeps, the door jars, and the window creaks, the old bench runs around the house, the walnut tree sheds its leaves, and so I molt all my feathers."

"Then," said the little girl, "I'll spill the milk." So she dropped the pitcher and spilled all the milk.

Now there was an old man just by on the top of a ladder thatching a rick, and when he saw the little girl spill the milk, he said, "Little girl, what do you mean by spilling the milk? Your little brothers and sisters must go without their supper."

Then said the little girl, "Titty's dead, and Tatty weeps, the stool hops, and the broom sweeps, the door jars, and the window creaks, the old bench runs around the house, the walnut tree sheds its leaves, the little bird molts its feathers, and so I spill the milk."

"Oh!" said the old man, "Then I'll tumble off the ladder and break my neck." So he tumbled off the ladder and broke his neck. And when the old man broke his neck, the great walnut tree fell down with a crash, and upset the old bench and house, and the house falling knocked the window out, and the window knocked the door down, and the door upset the broom, and the broom upset the stool, and poor little Tatty Mouse was buried beneath the ruins.

OLD SULTAN

Grimm Brothers

There was once a faithful sheepdog called Sultan who had grown old and lost all his teeth. One day Sultan's master stood outside his cottage with his wife and shook his head sadly.

"I'll have to shoot Old Sultan. He isn't any use anymore."

"Please don't shoot him, husband. He's been a good friend all these years. He can't live much longer so let's look after him."

"He's useless," said the shepherd crossly. "He can't even round up the sheep. No, tomorrow he must go." Poor Sultan was lying on the step and overheard every word. He was terrified. To think he had only one day left to live! That evening he crept off to visit his friend the wolf in the nearby wood. "Unhappy me," he barked. "My master plans to shoot me tomorrow."

"Don't worry," growled the wolf, "this is what

144

we must do. Your shepherd and his wife always take their little boy with them when they go up to the field. They leave him by the shady hedge while they get on with their work. I'll run out of this wood, snatch him up and run away with him. You must chase after me just as fast as you can. When I drop him, you must pick him up. After that, you gently carry him back and his parents will be certain you've rescued their child from a wicked wolf – me!"

"What a clever idea," Sultan woofed, "thank you, old friend."

Well, everything went as they had planned. The wolf ran away with boy and while the shepherd and his wife screamed Sultan raced along and caught up with the wolf then carried the poor child back.

"You've saved my son's life," the shepherd said, patting Sultan's head. "Your life must be spared. Go home, dear wife, and prepare a good dinner for this faithful friend and give him my soft blanket too." From that day, Sultan lived very comfortably indeed.

Soon afterward, the wolf visited Sultan. "I have a favor to ask. I'd like you to turn your head the other way whenever I want to enjoy eating one of the shepherd's fine lambs."

"I couldn't do that," replied Sultan, "my master trusts me." The wolf didn't believe Sultan but when he sneaked in to steal a lamb, the shepherd was waiting with a heavy stick to chase him away.

Sultan had told him about the wolf's plans in good time.

The wolf was furious. He promised to be revenged so he sent a huge boar to challenge Sultan to a fight. Sultan asked the shepherd's three-legged cat to go with him but the poor creature walked so awkwardly that her tail stuck straight up into air.

When the wolf and the boar saw their enemy approaching through the grass, they saw the cat's tail sticking straight up and they were sure it was a mighty sword for Sultan to use. Then when the poor cat bobbed unevenly on her three legs, they thought she was picking up stones to hurl at them.

"Swords, stones. We can't fight like that," they whispered, so the wolf leap up a tree and the boar hid behind a bush.

"Where have they gone? asked Sultan.

"I don't know," replied the cat, "but I think I have spotted a mouse. And she pounced! Oh dear,

the boar's ears were sticking up above his hiding place. When he twitched one of them, the cat scratched and tried to drag it out. The boar grunted in pain and sprang up. "There's the one you should be biting," he roared. They looked up and sure enough, they spotted the wolf.

"Scared of an old dog and a three-legged cat, are you?" they laughed. Shamefaced, the wolf crept down. He shook Sultan's paw and promised to be his good friend from then on.

THE UGLY DUCKLING

Hans Christian Andersen

One summer, when the corn was golden yellow and the hay was being dried in the fields, a mother duck was sitting on her nest of eggs. She sat in the rushes of a deep moat that surrounded a lovely country manor and waited for her eggs to hatch. It was taking a very long time and she was getting very tired.

At last, one day she felt a movement beneath her. The eggs began to crack and out popped tiny fluffy ducklings. All the eggs hatched except for one, which was larger than the rest. The mother duck was impatient to take her new ducklings swimming but could not leave the last egg unhatched. She sat for a few more days, and just as she was about to give up, she heard a tapping and out of the shell tumbled the oddest, ugliest duckling she had ever seen.

She took the babies into the water and proudly watched as they all swam straightaway, even the ugly duckling. She led them in a procession around the moat, showing them off to the other ducks. As they bobbed behind her she heard many quacks of admiration and praise for her fine family. But she also heard laughter and scorn poured on the ugly duckling at the end of the line.

"He has been too long in the egg," she explained, "he has not come out quite the right shape. But he is strong and will grow into a fine duck soon."

As the weeks went by, and the corn was harvested in the fields, the ducklings grew up into ducks. But the ugly duckling with his gray feathers and clumsy shape remained different. All the ducks on the moat pecked him and made fun of him and refused to let him join in their games on the water.

At last the ugly duckling could bear it no more. As the fall leaves began to fall he flew away to a great marsh. There he stayed alone, hiding from the ducks among the reeds.

One day, he heard a strange cry and the sound of wings in the air. Looking up he saw three dazzling white birds flying majestically overhead. The ugly duckling felt a strange longing. He did not know the name of those birds but he felt he loved them more than he had loved anything before. He watched as they passed over his head and flew beyond until they were out of sight.

Fall turned to winter, and the ugly duckling suffered many hardships.

The marshy water froze over with the cold weather and the poor duckling became trapped fast in the ice. A kind man happened to come by and he saw that he was in trouble. He broke the ice with his shoe and freed the duckling and carried him to his home. His children made a great fuss of the duckling and wanted to take hold of him. But the ugly duckling was frightened and flapped his wings in alarm. He upset a bucket of milk and fled as people ran after him shouting.

He struggled through many other difficulties during his first winter, but at last spring came, and with it warm sunshine. The ugly duckling felt better than he had done for months and flapped his wings. To his surprise they felt bigger and stronger, and he found he was flying easily away from the marsh towards a large and beautiful lake.

He alighted on the water and saw before him the three wonderful birds he had seen flying overhead several months before. As the swans glided smoothly over the lake, the ugly duckling felt drawn to them, but he was sure they would peck and tease him like the ducks because he was so ugly.

At last he thought, "It's better to be hurt by birds as lovely as these than to be teased by those ducks," and he floated slowly toward them. "Peck me, peck me," he whispered as he drew nearer and he bent his neck in shame.

All at once he saw a reflection in the smooth lake waters. A beautiful swan with glossy white feathers and a fine yellow beak stared up at him. He moved; the swan moved. He opened his wings; so did the swan. The ugly duckling suddenly realized – he was a swan.

The other swans swam gracefully toward him, welcoming him and stroking him with their beaks. Some children came running down to the lake and called out to their father.

"Look a new swan has appeared. He is more beautiful than any of the others!" The children clapped their hands together in delight and they threw pieces of bread into the water for him.

The young and beautiful swan felt quite shy with all this attention, and hid his head under his wing. But, as the lilac trees bent their branches down to the water and the sun shone warm and bright, he felt a deep happiness. He rustled his feathers, arched his

sleek long neck, and said to himself, "I never dreamed of such great happiness when I was the Ugly Duckling."

THE RAVEN
AND THE FOX

Aesop

"This is the life," thought Raven and indeed it was. The sun stood high in a cloudless sky and there was hardly a breath of wind. It was perfect flying weather and if there was one thing Raven enjoyed it was flying. He soared up and up on warm currents of air, then tumbled down through the sky. He did nose-dives ("beak-dives," he called them) and even flew upside down.

"Show off," chirped Sparrow to Thrush as they watched. "Thinks he's something special. Just look at the way he flies; like a huge black bull in the sky."

Unfortunately for Sparrow, Raven heard this.

"Pruk, pruk," he croaked. "How dare you say that!"

Raven had a very deep voice and he sounded very cross.

"Idiot!" screeched Thrush. "What if he sees our cake?"

It was too late. Raven had already seen it. Now if there was one thing Raven enjoyed more than flying it was strawberry cheesecake. One nose dive later he had it in his beak and away he flew, leaving Sparrow and Thrush twittering helplessly.

Raven perched in a majestic oak, feeling like a king. After some splendid flying here he was, deliciously cool and comfortable, with a large slice of strawberry cheesecake in his beak. And it was lunchtime.

"Ahem. I mean, ahem." Fox cleared his throat to get Raven's attention. His cough also hid the rumble of his tummy. His nose had caught the scent of something which made his mouth water and he had found the right tree in a flash.

"My dear Raven," said Fox in a voice of silk and honey. "How simply delightful to see you. You look lovely. Indeed, you always do. Just to see your brilliant black plumage shining in the sun is enough to make a fox happy. How lucky you are, the most skillful, intelligent, and good-looking bird around."

"Pruk, pruk," croaked Raven. "My dear Fox, how nice of you to say so, thank you." But of course he could hardly croak at all because of the enormous piece of cheesecake in his beak.

"Stone the crows," said Fox. "You sound dreadful. I'm so sorry. You used to have such a fine voice too."

Now Raven was very proud of his voice. It was deep and strong, and to prove that there was nothing wrong with it he opened his beak wide and began to sing. Which was a big mistake, because the strawberry cheesecake fell, faster than the fastest beak-dive, straight into Fox's mouth. By the time Raven realized what had happened, Fox and the strawberry cheesecake had gone. Raven felt terrible. In the end he had nothing to crow about.

For permission to reproduce copyright material
acknowledgment and thanks are due to the following:

Faber and Faber Ltd. for "How the Polar Bear Became"
from *How the Whale Became and Other Stories* by Ted
Hughes. Walker Books Ltd. for *Tigers Forever* by
Ruskin Bond (© 1983 Ruskin Bond).

Stories retold from traditional sources that in this
version are © Grisewood & Dempsey Ltd. are as
follows: "The Hare and the Tortoise", "The Lioness
and the Mouse", and "The Raven and the Fox" are
retold by Robin Lister. "Why the Raven has Black
Feathers", "Billy Bear's Stumpy Tale", "The Three
Billy Goats Gruff", "Henny Penny", "The Two
Frogs", "Titty Mouse and Tatty Mouse", and "Old
Sultan" are retold by Nora Clarke. "Brer Rabbit Gets
Himself a House" and "The Ugly Duckling" are retold
by Linda Yeatman. "The Seal Catcher" and "The
Ostrich and the Hedgehog" are retold by Eugenie
Summerfield.

Every effort has been made to obtain permission from
copyright holders. If, regrettably, any omissions have
been made, we shall be pleased to make suitable
corrections in any reprint.